THE DARK CITY

CATHERINE FISHER

RELIC MASTER

THE DARK CITY

Dial Books

an imprint of Penguin Group (USA) Inc.

DIAL BOOKS

An imprint of Penguin Group (USA) Inc.

Published by The Penguin Group

Penguin Group (USA) Inc., 375 Hudson Street, New York, NY 10014, U.S.A.

Penguin Group (Canada), 90 Eglinton Avenue East, Suite 700, Toronto, Ontario, Canada M4P 2Y3 (a division of Pearson Penguin Canada Inc.) • Penguin Books Ltd, 80 Strand, London WC2R 0RL, England • Penguin Ireland, 25 St. Stephen's Green, Dublin 2, Ireland (a division of Penguin Books Ltd) • Penguin Group (Australia), 250 Camberwell Road, Camberwell, Victoria 3124, Australia (a division of Pearson Australia Group Pty Ltd) • Penguin Books India Pvt Ltd, 11 Community Centre, Panchsheel Park, New Delhi - 110 017, India • Penguin Group (NZ), 67 Apollo Drive, Rosedale, Auckland 0632, New Zealand (a division of Pearson New Zealand Ltd) • Penguin Books (South Africa) (Pty) Ltd, 24 Sturdee Avenue, Rosebank, Johannesburg 2196, South Africa • Penguin Books Ltd, Registered Offices: 80 Strand, London WC2R 0RL, England

First published in the United States 2011 by Dial Books
Published in the United Kingdom 1998 by Random House Children's Books
Copyright © 1998 by Catherine Fisher
Designed by Nancy R. Leo-Kelly
Text set in Sabon
Printed in the U. S. A.
1 3 5 7 9 10 8 6 4 2

Library of Congress Cataloging-in-Publication Data
Fisher, Catherine, date.
The dark city / by Catherine Fisher.
p. cm. — (Relic Master ; [1])
Summary: Sixteen-year-old Raffi, Master Galen, and a mysterious traveler, Carys,
enter the ruined city of Tasceron seeking a relic that may save the world, while evading
the Watch, a brutal organization opposed to the Order to which Raffi and Galen belong.
ISBN 978-0-8037-3673-3 (hardcover)
[1. Fantasy. 2. Apprentices—Fiction. 3. Antiquities—Fiction.] I. Title.
PZ7.F4995 Dam 2011 [Fic]—dc22

To Stephen Herrington
for the idea

Contents

THE DARK CITY

The Box of Flames

1

The world is not dead. The world is alive and breathes. The world is the whim of God, and her journey is forever.

Litany of the Makers

THE SEVEN MOONS were all in the sky at once. Tonight they made the formation that Galen called the web: one in the center—Pyra, the small red one—and the others in a circle around her. They glimmered over the treetops; it was a good omen, the sisters' most perfect dance.

Raffi stared up at them with his arms full of wood. As an experiment, he let his third eye open and made tiny purple filaments of light spray from the central moon to all the others, linking them in a flaring pattern. After a while he changed the color to blue, managing to hold it for a few minutes, and even when it faded, a faint echo still lingered. He watched it till his arms were tired, then he held the wood more carefully and turned away.

That had been better than last time. He was getting quite good at it—he ought to tell Galen.

Or maybe not.

Gathering up more of the crumbling twigs, he moved through the dark trees resentfully. It was no use talking to Galen. The keeper was in one of his bitter moods; he'd only laugh, that short, harsh laugh of contempt.

The wood was very dry, rotting on the forest floor. Huge ants scurried out of it, and the armored wood-grubs that chewed slowly. He flicked a shower of them from his clothes.

The forest was quiet. Two nights ago a pack of woses had raged through here, tearing great holes in the leaf canopy; the wreckage still lay under the oaks. In the green gloom of the night, insects hummed; something whistled behind him in the wood. It was time he was getting back.

He pushed through hanging ivies and across a clearing deep in bracken, alert for snakes and the venomous blue spiders, but only shadows shifted and blurred among the trees, too far off to see or sense. He'd come farther than he'd thought and in the shafts of moonlight, red and pale and rose, the path looked unfamiliar, until the trees ended in a bank of dead leaves. He waded through them to the hillside, seeing the vast black hump of the cromlech and Galen's fire like a spark in its shadow.

Then he stopped.

Somewhere behind him, far behind, something had tripped one of the sense-lines. The warning tweaked a tiny pain over one eye; he recognized it at once. The lines were well above ground; whatever it was, it was big, and coming this way. He listened, intent, but only the night sounds came to him, the insect buzz and the flittermice, the crackle of the fire.

Scattering wood, he ran down quickly.

"What's the matter?" Galen sat carelessly against the slabs of the tomb, his coat tugged tight around him. "Scared of moths now?"

Raffi dumped the wood in a heap; dust rose from it. "One of the sense-lines just snapped!"

The keeper stared at him for a moment. Then he turned

to the fire and began piling the wood onto the flames. "Did it now."

"Don't do that! Someone might be coming!"

Galen shrugged. "Let them."

"It could be anyone!" Raffi dropped to a crouch, almost sick with worry, the strings of purple and blue stones he wore around his neck swinging. He caught hold of them. "It could be the Watch! Put the fire out at least!"

Galen paused. When he looked up, his face was a mask of flame light and haggard shadows, his deep eyes barely gleaming, his hook nose exaggerated like a hawk's. "No," he said harshly. "If they want me, let them come. I've had enough of skulking in the dark." He eased his left leg with both hands. "What direction?"

"West."

"From the mountains." He mused. "Could just be a traveler."

"Maybe." Raffi was preoccupied. Another line had twanged in his skull, closer now.

Galen watched him. "So. Let's put my pupil through his paces."

"What, now!"

10

"No better time." He turned his lean face to the fire. "If it is an enemy, what might we put on the flames?"

Raffi, appalled, rubbed his hair. He was scared now; he hated Galen in this mood. "Bitterwort. Scumweed, if we had any, goldenrod to make him sleepy. Shall I do that?"

"Do nothing, unless I tell you. Say nothing." Sharply, Galen raised his head, his profile dark against the smallest moon. "Have you got the blue box?"

Raffi nodded; he clutched it, in his pocket.

"Use it only if the danger is extreme."

"I know, I know. But—"

A twig snapped. Somewhere nearby a were-bird shrieked and flew off through the branches. Behind it, Raffi caught the snuffle of a horse.

He stood up, heart thumping. Behind him the cromlech was black and solid, the rock face gnarled under his palms, hollowed by a thousand years of frost and rain. Lichen grew on it, a green powder over the faint carved spirals. It felt like a great beast, fossilized and hunched.

Galen pulled himself up too, without his stick. His

long hair swung forward, the tangled strings of black jet-stones and green crystal catching the light, the heavy cowl of his coat high around his neck.

"Ready?" he breathed.

"I think so."

The keeper gave him a scornful glance. "Don't worry. I won't risk your life."

"It's not mine I'm worried about." But Raffi muttered it sullenly under his breath, feeling for the powders and the blue box.

A horse came abruptly out of the wood.

It was tall, one of the thin, red-painted kinds they bred beyond the mountains, and the sweat on its long, skeletal neck made it ghostly in the sisters' light. It walked forward and stopped just beyond the flicker of the fire. Staring into the dark, Raffi could just make out the rider: a dim, bulky figure muffled against the cold.

No one spoke.

Raffi glanced into the trees. He couldn't sense anyone else. He tried to look into the wood with his third eye, but he was too nervous; only shadows moved. The rider stirred.

"A fine evening, friends." His voice was deep; a big man.

Galen nodded, his long dark hair swinging. "So it is. You've come far?"

"Far enough."

The horse shifted, its harness clinking softly. The rider urged it a few steps forward, perhaps to see them better.

"Come to the fire," Galen said dangerously.

The horse's fear was tangible, a smell on the air. It was terrified of the cromlech, or perhaps the invisible web of earth-lines that ran out from it. The man, too, sounded tense when he spoke again. "I don't think so, keepers."

Galen's voice was quiet as he answered. "That's an unlucky title. Why should we be keepers?"

"This is an unlucky place. Who else would be living here?" The rider hesitated, then swung himself down from the saddle and came forward a few steps, unwinding a filmy, knitted wrapping from his face.

They saw a powerful, thick-set man, black-bearded. A crossbow of some sort was slung on his shoulder. He wore a metal breastplate too; it gleamed in the light of the moons. Dangerous, Raffi thought. But nothing they couldn't handle.

The stranger must have thought the same. "I bring no threat here," he went on quickly. "How could I? There's no doubt an armory of sorcery aimed at me as I stand." He held up both hands, empty; a jewel gleamed on the left gauntlet. "I'm looking for a man named Galen Harn, a Relic Master." He glanced at Raffi, expressionless. "And for his scholar, Raffael Morel."

"Are you now," Galen said bleakly. He shifted; Raffi knew that his leg would be aching, but the keeper's face was hard. "And what do you want with them?"

"To pass on a message. West of here, about twenty leagues, in the foothills where the rivers meet, there's a settlement. The people there need him."

"Why?"

The rider smiled wryly, but he answered. "They found a relic, as they were plowing. A tube. When you touch it, it hums. Small green lights move inside it."

Galen didn't flicker, but Raffi knew he was alert. The horseman knew too. "It seems to me," he said ironically, "that if you should see this Galen, you might tell him.

The people are desperate that he come and deal with the thing. None of them dares go near it."

Galen nodded. "I'm sure. But the Order of keepers is outlawed. They're all either dead or in hiding from the Watch. If they're caught they face torture. This man might suspect a trap."

"He'd be safe enough." The rider scratched his beard and tried a step forward. "We need him. We wouldn't betray him. We're loyal to the old Order. That's all I can say, master. He'd just have to trust us."

Take one more step, Raffi thought. In his pocket his fingers trembled on the blue crystal box. He'd never used it on a man. Not yet.

The rider was still, as if he felt the tension.

Suddenly Galen moved, limping forward out of the tomb's shadow into the red and gold of the firelight. He stood tall, his face dark. "Tell them we'll come. Bury the device in the earth till we get there. Set a guard and let no one come near it. It may be dangerous."

The rider smiled. "Thank you. I'll see that it's done." He turned and climbed heavily up onto the horse; the red beast circled warily. "When can we expect you?"

"When we get there." Galen stared at him levelly. "I'd ask you to stay the night, but outlaws have little to share."

"Nor would I, keeper. Not under those stones." He turned away, then paused, glancing back. "The people will be glad to hear this. Depend upon it: You'll be safe with us. Ask for Alberic."

Then the horse stalked cautiously into the wood.

They both stood silent a long time, listening to the faint crackle and rustle, the distant charring of disturbed birds. The sense-lines snagged, one by one, in Raffi's head.

Finally, Galen moved. He sat down, hissing through his teeth with the stiffness of his leg. "Well. What do you think of that?"

Raffi took his hand off the blue box and collapsed beside him. Suddenly he felt unbearably tired. "That he's got guts, coming out here."

"And his story?"

"I don't know." He shrugged "It sounds true. But . . ."

"But. Exactly." The keeper sat back, his face in shadow.

"It could be a trap," Raffi ventured.

"So it could."

"But you're going anyway."

The Box of Flames

Galen laughed sourly. A sudden spark lit his face, twisted with pain. "I used to know when people lied to me, Raffi. If only they knew!" He glanced across. "We both go. Someone has to deal with this relic."

Uneasy, Raffi shook his head. "There may be no relic."

Galen spat into the fire. "What do I care," he said softly.

2

*This is how the world came to be. The
Makers came from the sky, on stairways
of ice. Flain opened his hands and the
land and sea were there, the soil and salt.
He set them one against the other, erod-
ing, in conflict forever. Out of stillness he
brought movement, out of peace, war.*

*Soren called out the leaves and the
trees. She walked the world, and seeds
fell from her sleeves and the hem of her
dress. The Woman of Leaves clothed the
world in a green brocade.*

*It was Tamar, the bearded one, who
brought the beasts. Down the silver stairs
he led them, the smallest a night-cub that
struggled in his arms.*

*All the sons of God watched them
scatter.*

Book of the Seven Moons

THE JOURNEY TO THE SETTLEMENT took five days. On his own, Raffi could have gotten there in four, but Galen's limp slowed them down. The keeper's leg was long healed, but it was stiff, and he walked grim and silent with a tall black stick. Even when the pain must have been bad after a long day's tramp in the rain or cold, he never talked about it. Raffi was used to it all: the keeper's brooding, his sudden outbreaks of foul temper. At times like these he kept quiet and wary and out of reach of the black stick. Galen had been hurt too deeply. The explosion had damaged more than his leg—it had scarred his mind. Toiling up the steep rocky path, the pack heavy on his shoulders, Raffi watched the Relic Master scramble ahead of him, slithering on scree. Galen was almost as unstable. And now this message.

If it was a trap, Galen wouldn't care. Raffi knew that sometimes he wanted to get caught, that he took deliberate risks, carelessly, proudly; like in the summer when they'd walked out of the forest into a village and taken a room and stayed there for three days, sleeping on comfortable beds, eating outside in full view of everyone. Galen hadn't cared, but for Raffi it had been three days of terror. The villagers hadn't betrayed them. Most had looked the other way. They'd been so lucky, Raffi thought, stumbling over a stone. Everyone knew there was a reward for the capture of any keeper. Two thousand marks. They'd been incredibly lucky.

"Come on!" Galen was standing on the top of the ridge. His voice was a growl through his teeth. "You can go faster than this. Don't think you need to slow down for me."

Raffi stopped, wiping sweat from his hair. "I'm not. The pack's heavy."

Galen glared at him. "Then give it to me."

The Box of Flames

"You've had your turn."

"Do you think I can't manage another?"

"I didn't say that!" Raffi spread his hands. "I just—"

"Save it! And move. We want to get to this place before night." He had turned and gone before Raffi could answer.

Looking at the empty sky, Raffi felt furious and hurt and reckless. For a cold moment, he told himself he would leave tonight, just take his things and go home. There were no Relic Masters now, the Order was broken. And Galen could look after himself with his scornful, bitter jealousy. But even as he raged, Raffi knew it all meant nothing, and he took the blue crystal box out and glared at it. Curiosity would keep him here. There was so much he had to learn. And he'd felt the power surge in him, and now he could never be without it.

THAT AFTERNOON they sat on warm stones on a hillside, looking down, at last, on the settlement.

"Well," Galen said acidly. "Well, well." He drank from the water flask and passed it over; Raffi took a cold mouthful thoughtfully. They had expected a village. And indeed there were houses, barns, outbuildings. But mostly, this was a fortress.

The central building was ancient; maybe even from the time of the Makers. The sides were strangely smooth and pale, the signs of old windows clear, now clumsily bricked up to slits. There were about six levels. On the higher ones balconies hung out precariously; most were ruined, but Raffi could see bowmen on one, tiny moving figures. The roof had partly collapsed, and been mended with hurdles and thatch.

"What do you think?" He passed the flask back and chewed the hard bread. "Safe?"

"Not safe." Galen stared down moodily. "Those who have the nerve to live in a Maker-house are no ordinary villagers. Since the Emperor fell the land has gone wild. Robber-gangs, warlords, each one fighting the others. I'm sure this is the castle of one such."

"And we're going in, blindly."

Galen gave a sour grin. "Going in, yes. Blindly, no."

The stones were warm in the autumn sun. Raffi leaned back, feeling better somehow. "Sense-lines?"

The Box of Flames

"Around us both. Powders. And if all else fails, the box."

Raffi shook his head. "If there are too many of them, that won't save us. It might be better not to go in at all."

"Curiosity, Raffi. Always my downfall." Galen was rummaging in the pack; now he brought out a small black tube and held it in both hands lovingly. He spoke a prayer, and made the sign of humility. Then he put the tube to his eye and looked down.

Like the blue box, it was a relic, a holy thing the Makers had left. They had found it in a farm north of the forest two years ago; the woman of the place had sent for them secretly, terrified the Watch would find out. Galen had blessed the farm, spoken prayers over the house, and taken the relic away. He had a secret place to keep them, a cave in the hills. Once, coming back there, they had found signs on the walls, as if some other member of the Order might have sheltered there. But the marks had been rain-washed, unclear. No one knew how many of the Order were even alive.

Galen gazed at the tower for a long time. Then he handed the tube to Raffi, who stared. "Me?"

"Why not. It's time you did."

Nervous, Raffi took it. It was warm and miraculously smooth, made of the Makers' strange material, not wood or stone or skin, the secret no one knew. He muttered a prayer over it, then raised it and looked in.

Despite himself he gasped.

The fortress was huge, close up. He saw the weeds growing from it, the cracks in the walls. The door was bricked up, a small black slot where two men loitered, talking. He moved the tube carefully; noted the deep pits, the spiked ditch, the strong fence with the walkway behind it.

"Whoever they are, they're well-defended."

"Indeed." Galen's voice sounded amused. "Now touch the red button."

He felt for it; the tube stretched itself in his fingers, the focus blurring quickly to his eyesight. Houses and a row of stalls, their goods hanging in the wind, tawdry and cheap. Dogs in the mud. A crowd of women washing clothes in tubs. Smoke. He followed it up, high into the sky, until the small moon Agramon flashed briefly across the glass. For a moment even that looked close, the smooth faint surface, with tiny formations glinting.

The Box of Flames

"That's enough!" Galen's hand clasped around the tube; Raffi let go reluctantly. The Relic Master folded it into its wrappings, pushed it deep in the sack, and stood up.

Suddenly he looked dangerous, his gaunt face tense, his eyes dark under deep brows. "Come on," he said grimly. "Let's go and ask for Alberic."

IT WAS NIGHT when they reached the gates, and the buildings glimmered behind the palisade. The men stationed outside had a lantern; they were playing dice, but they stood up soon enough.

Galen ignored them. He strode past without a word, through the open gates, and no one challenged him. Hurrying behind, Raffi glanced back; the men were whispering. Planning to shut us in, he thought.

They walked together between the dark houses, through the mud, the soft pools of water and dung. The stench of the place was appalling. Filthy children watched them from doorways, silent and unsmiling. The buildings were squalid and patched, the wood rotten and green

27

with age. As he squelched through the muck, Galen muttered, "Anything?"

"People watching. Just curious." The sense-lines moved about them, invisible, fluid. Raffi held them with some distant part of his mind, easily, from long practice. It had been the first thing Galen had taught him.

The fortress loomed up. Noise and smoke drifted out from it, laughter, the yells of an argument. In the ruined windows, faint lights glimmered; the strange smooth walls were dappled with moonlight.

At the doorway, the entrance Raffi had seen through the glass, three men waited. Their weapons were in their hands—long hooked knives. They watched Galen come with a mixture of fear and something else, something disturbing. Warnings rippled in Raffi's skull. "Galen . . ."

But Galen had walked right up to them.

"My name is Galen Harn. I'm looking for Alberic."

Whatever else, they weren't surprised. One grinned at the others. "We've been expecting you, keeper. Come with me."

Inside was dark, a maze of rooms and passages. Voices echoed ahead, or from behind closed doors;

28

smoky torches guttered on brackets. The air was fetid and smelled worse than outside. As they walked down a long corridor, men squeezed past them, a few slaves, two girls giggling behind Raffi's back, sending the sense-lines rippling. Looking up, he saw something on a wall, marks under the dirt, a symbol he knew. Next to it was a grid of buttons and numbers by a door. Galen stopped too and made the humility sign; Raffi knew he longed to touch it. "This is a relic," he said to their guide. "It shouldn't be left here."

The man shrugged easily. "That's up to Alberic."

"Don't you fear it?"

"I stay away from it, keeper. The whole castle is old."

"Where does this door lead?"

"Nowhere. There's a square shaft behind it, empty. Goes right down." He leered. "Alberic uses it as a burial pit. Knee-deep in skeletons."

He wasn't joking. Raffi glanced at Galen, but the keeper's face was dark and grim. Putting his hand in his pocket, he let the touch of the blue box comfort him.

They came to some stairs leading up, wide but dingy. Raffi's eyes smarted from the smoke; he stumbled on greasy bones and other rubbish in the thick straw. Gnats whined around him; fleas too, he didn't doubt.

The stairs rose up. Ahead in the dark, Galen climbed them steadily, his black stick tapping. Something was cooking somewhere, a rich, meaty smell that tormented Raffi like a pain. He wondered if they'd get any of it. He couldn't remember when he'd last eaten meat.

Finally they came to the top, a long, dim room, full of smoke. The floor was made of wooden planks, sanded smooth; it spread before them, an empty expanse.

Their guide stood still. "Go on," he said curtly.

Through the smoke they saw a group of four people waiting for them, sitting and standing around a fire at the far end of the room. Galen glanced across. "Well?"

"It doesn't feel right."

The keeper shrugged. "Too late." He stalked forward; Raffi followed him down the hall, his heart hammering with nerves.

Talk hushed. The men and woman waiting stood up, all but one, the man in the center. As Raffi came closer, he saw to his astonishment that the man was tiny, his feet resting on a box, his body far too small for the great cushioned chair in which he sat. His face was narrow and clever, his hair stubbly; he wore a gold collar and a green quilted jacket slashed with red.

Galen stood still, and looked down at him. "I was told to ask for Alberic," he said gravely.

The dwarf nodded, his eyes sharp. "You've found him," he replied.

3

*Though the Makers are gone, their relics
remain. Let the keepers seek them out.
For the power in them is holy.*

Litany of the Makers

I T WAS A TRAP.

Raffi knew that, as soon as he saw Alberic. He had a
sudden vivid sense of the empty room behind him, the
stairs, the maze of corridors, the gate and spikes and
ditches. It was a trap, and they were well inside it.

But Alberic only grinned. "So you're Galen Harn. You
took some finding."

Galen said nothing. His face was stern.

"And a pupil!" The dwarf's shrewd eyes glanced over
Raffi. "Bursting with sorceries, no doubt."

Someone sniggered behind him. Alberic leaned back
into the cushions, the candlelight soft on the silk of

35

his jerkin. "Sit down, please," he said amiably.

A big, black-haired man lifted a gilt chair from the wall and thumped it down in front of Galen. As he straightened up, he smirked at them and they recognized the horseman from the forest. He still wore the breastplate; close up it looked thin, pitted with rust.

Galen ignored the chair. Someone edged a small stool toward Raffi, and he gave it a longing glance but stayed standing.

"We came here," Galen said ominously, "because of your message. A relic . . ."

"Ah yes!" The small man put his tiny fingers together and grinned over them. "I'm afraid there might have been a slight misunderstanding there." He gave the briefest of nods. The sense-lines snapped; Raffi found himself being shoved onto the stool by a girl in snaky armor, and glancing around he saw they had forced Galen to sit too, the black-bearded man and another standing over him.

For a moment the keeper's eyes were black with fury. Then he seemed to control himself; he leaned back, thrusting his legs out.

The Box of Flames

"You seem determined to make us comfortable."

"It's not that. I don't like looking up."

They stared at each other. Finally the dwarf's grin widened. He spread his hands. "It's like this, keeper. I'm the power here. My body may be puny, but my brain's sharp, sharper than any, and my lads and lasses here know Alberic's plans and Alberic's cunning bring the most gold. This is Sikka, Godric, whom you've already met, and Taran. My rogues, my children."

He blew a kiss at them; the girl Sikka laughed, and Taran, a man in a dirty blue coat, gave a snort of derision. Carefully, Raffi moved his hand an inch toward his pocket.

"Gold." Galen nodded. "So you're thieves, then."

There was a tense silence. Raffi went cold all over. Then Alberic shook his head. "For a wise man you have a blunt tongue, Galen. As it is, this time I'll let you keep it." He leaned over and poured himself a drink from a delicate glass container on a round table beside him, lit by tall candles. The goblet glittered; it was crystal, almost priceless. Raffi tightened his dry lips. Slowly Alberic drank, leaning back on the plump cushions.

"The relic," Galen growled.

"There is no relic. At least—" The small man sat up, looking around in mock surprise. "I don't think so. Is there?"

The girl laughed. "You're a cruel man, Alberic," she said, coming around and gripping the back of his carven chair. She stared at Galen in amusement. "Did you really believe that we'd have a terror of relics, like the old fools in the villages?"

Galen said nothing; it was Alberic who answered. "Oh no," he said softly, watching the Relic Master. "Oh no, my pet, he's a deeper one than that. Very deep. I think he knew what he was coming into all along. I think he knew very well . . ."

For a moment the dwarf's voice was so thoughtful that Raffi had the sudden sense he had guessed Galen's bitter secret, and his anxiety sent the sense-lines rippling, so that he had to fight to hold on to them. Alberic watched silently, head on one side. Suddenly his voice was sharp. "Let me see some sorcery, keeper. I need to know you're who you say you are, not some spy of the Watch."

Galen's hands tightened, the fingers clenching on the chair. Raffi saw them uneasily.

The Box of Flames

"I don't do sorcery—as you call it—on the orders of anyone." His face was proud and his dark stern eyes held Alberic's. "I'm a Relic Master of the Order of keepers, and the power I have is holy. Not for fireside tricks."

Alberic nodded. "But the Order is finished," he said sweetly. "Broken, outlawed. Dead."

"The power remains." Galen leaned back in his chair, legs stretched out. He had the look of a man playing chess, playing for his life, on an invisible board.

"To open and close," Alberic murmured, "build and destroy, see forward and back."

Raffi looked surprised; Galen didn't. The dwarf grinned at them. "One of your Order was once . . . in the way, on one of our raids. Unfortunately some of my rogues were a little enthusiastic. The only thing he had worth stealing was the Litany of the Makers, written in code on parchment. I worked it out and read it. An amusement for the long winter nights . . ."

Galen said nothing, his eyes cold with anger.

"The boy, then!" Alberic waved at Raffi. "Let the boy do something. You don't object to that?"

Galen shrugged. "If he wants to. He knows little. A

few effects of light that might amuse you." He turned a cold look on Raffi. "Do your best for our audience."

Reluctantly Raffi stood up, catching the hidden message. They all stared at him, and he felt nervous and furious with Galen. But then, he'd had no choice.

He stepped out and pushed the stool away with his foot. Then he raised both hands, spoke the words in his mind, and let his third eye open, the eye of the Makers.

In the air he made the seven moons, each hanging from nothing, the small red Pyra, pitted Cyrax, the icy globe of Atterix, all the sisters of the old Book. They glowed in the dark room, and beyond them he glimpsed Alberic, watching intently, his face bright with the dappled lights.

"Very pretty," the dwarf murmured. "Most pleasing."

But he hardly seemed impressed. Uneasy, Raffi set the globes spinning. They moved in long ellipses, made the complex orbits of the moons, each leaving a glinting thread of light that interwove into a net of colors, purples and reds and blues. And each had its own note of music that hummed, building into harmonies that rose and gathered in the dim hall, an underthrob of sound like the voices of strange beings. He was sweating now, and there was a pain behind his eyes, but he kept the moons spinning till the wordless song rose to a crescendo of exquisite beauty, and then he let it fade, slowly, into silence. The moons became ghosts of light. Then they were gone.

"Charming," Alberic said drily.

Sweating, his head thumping, Raffi glanced at Galen. He hadn't moved but sat still, arms folded. "Is that enough for you?"

"Certainly. No Watchman could do that. With such a pupil you must be who you say you are."

"You never doubted that."

Alberic grinned. "No."

"So what do you want? We're not worth robbing."

There was silence. Wearily Raffi sat down; no one took any notice of him. He slid his hand into his pocket and gripped the blue box. The tension in the room was taut as a rope; he could feel it tighten his nerves.

For the first time Alberic didn't seem amused. He drank from his glass and flashed a glance at the girl, Sikka. She nodded, her long plaited hair swinging.

The small man put his glass down. "Revenge. I want revenge."

"On us?"

Alberic smiled dangerously. "Don't pretend to be stupid." For a moment he fingered his golden collar, then he looked up and said fiercely, "You called us thieves. Indeed we are. What does a thief hate most, wise one?"

"To be robbed." Galen's voice was somber, his hawk-face a mask of shadows.

"Indeed." Alberic looked at him, impressed. "Let me tell you about it. Two months ago, a wandering Sekoi came to this place. He was one of the ones who tell stories: a lazy, mocking creature. Brindled gray and brown. A zigzag under one eye."

Raffi edged closer. Any mention of the Sekoi fascinated him. He had only seen a few of them, years ago when he'd been too small and had run away, thinking they would eat him. The Sekoi were the others, the different race. They were taller than men, and thin, their sharp faces furred like cats, their long fingers streaked in tribal markings. People said it was the Sekoi who had made the cromlechs, eons ago, before the Makers came. They had

stories about that time, or so Galen said. The Order had
had texts of a few, laboriously copied in the great library
in the tower of Karelian. All dust now.

"He fooled us," Alberic said waspishly. "Hung around,
played with the children. We threw him out but he came
back. He prattled, dreamed, sang foreign songs. We
thought he was harmless."

"The Sekoi make an art of that," Galen muttered.
He was looking at the jug of wine. Alberic noticed, and
grinned.

"As you say. All the time he was learning about us,
where the strongrooms were, who held the keys, what the
raids brought in." He shook his head. "There was plenty
of that, believe me. Gold, silver, clothes, wool, wine. This
place is well stuffed."

"I can believe it." Galen leaned back, pushing the long
hair from his face. "And so he robbed you."

The dwarf glared. "He gave a performance. Down
in the courtyard. None of us had seen a Sekoi work."
He leaned forward. "No disrespect to you, boy, but he
was astounding. He told a story, and the things he spoke
of appeared, and I was inside the story, we all were; it

happened all around us. It was some tale of castles and battles and gods who rode from the sky on silver horses, and believe me, keeper, I lived every minute of it! I felt the rain, the sparks from the swords, had to run out of the way in case I was crushed." He leaned back, remembering. "It was no illusion. It was real. Some of my people were injured in that dream. Two never came out of it."

"And when it ended?"

Alberic's eyes were hooded with wrath. "The fires out, the courtyard dark, the guards asleep. And the strongroom door wide open."

"What did he take?" Raffi asked eagerly.

"Gold. What do they ever want? A box of gold marks. A fortune!"

"You want it back."

"I want him!" Alberic leaped up suddenly, shoving Godric aside and prowling, a tiny, hunched figure, among the candles. "I want that filthy dream-peddler! What I'll do to him!" He spun, his eyes bright. "And then with him! Imagine the work he could do for me, the use he'd be to me. I want him brought back, relic-man. And I want you to get him."

The Box of Flames

Galen sat still, his black hair and clothes making him a figure of darkness. Raffi knew he was tense, uncertain.

"Why me?"

"You have ways. I'm known, so are my people. None of us can travel that far. The Watch . . ."

Galen laughed bitterly. "The Watch! They want me more than you. No, you can find the creature yourself, thief-lord. He may well be sharper than you are." Then, abruptly, he looked up. "Why did you think I would go?"

"Because of our hostage."

"What hostage?"

Alberic grinned at him. "The boy."

Raffi felt the sense-lines leap; danger surged in the room like a tide. "Galen!" he gasped, jumping up.

The stool smacked behind him. The blue box was in his hand. Weapons glinted; Godric's sword unsheathed with a sharp snick; Sikka caught hold of him so that he yelled and jerked the box up, his thumb stabbing the small round control.

The box throbbed. A blast of light scorched out from it, searing the floor at Alberic's feet so that the dwarf leaped back with a yell, the planks blackened and smoking. Shock forced Raffi back; the box jerked out of his hand and he grabbed for it but Alberic already had him, a knife jabbed in his ribs, one skinny hand gripping his hair so that he yelped in pain.

Through watering eyes he saw their astonished faces, the crisped ends of the straw stinking and curling. In front of him, Galen was holding the box level, his eyes bleak.

"Now that," Alberic said slowly, "is a relic worth having." He turned the knife in Raffi's side. "Even if you get out, the boy won't."

"Let him go."

"I might. If you give me that box." The dwarf stared at it greedily.

"Never." Galen was steady, without expression.

Alberic shrugged. "Your choice, keeper. Keep the box; lose the boy."

4

It is vital to remember that the powers the Order claim to have are a complete illusion.

Rule of the Watch

Journal of Carys Arrin
Atelgarsday
3.16.546

Two days ago, at last, I found the cromlech.

As I wrote in my last report, the people of the forest hate to talk to strangers; finding anything out is difficult. I'm still traveling as a pack-merchant, so bribes have been easy to give, but it's cost me a great deal in fabrics, buttons, agricultural tools. (NB—Claim the money for this when I get back.) The forest is an eerie place, and most of our charts of it are wrong. The old superstitions of the Order hang around here; also a number of fugitives and vagabonds. Other areas are empty. Once I traveled for three days down airless green paths, slashing my way through, and saw no one. Jekkles have attacked me twice—once scaring the pack-beast almost berserk. Fire seems to keep them off. There are also blue spiders that bite; as I write this my hand is swollen and black, but I killed the thing fast enough to save my life.

Once I'd found it, I watched the cromlech for three hours. No one came near it. Finally, wary for traps, I crawled out, gathered the pack-beasts together, and picked my way down. The slope was steep and rocky. Night was coming; strange mists and veils of murk clung around the rotting tree-stumps, and the enormous stones stood like shadows. As I clambered down to it, my whole skin prickled. The foul witcheries of the place hung on the air.

Someone had been living there, that was clear. There were fire-marks, a pit dug for rubbish, a lot of footprints. But the ashes of the fire were about a day old, and had already been scattered and scratched at by some animal. The Relic Master had gone.

There was no chance of following straight-away—twilight was closing and only four of the moons were up. Warily I wandered around, searching the ground carefully. The place is all humps and hollows; a green ditch surrounds the stones, and as I crossed it I thought I felt a whisper of power. Galen Harn and his boy were here. I'm close to them.

But there was one thing that puzzled me. In the soft mud near the forest fringe I found hoof prints. They came near, but stayed outside the ring. The horse had trampled the ground as if it had stood there and been restless for some time. Then it had gone, back among the trees.

Could Harn have gotten hold of a horse? Could it carry both of them? In one way it would make tracking them easier, but they would move fast then, faster than me.

Don't make problems, old Jellie used to say. Think things out, be clear, and always watch your back. I remembered that when I turned around.

The cromlech is huge, close up. One great lintel-stone balances on three others, the whole thing black against the sky. It must be thousands of years old. I don't know if there are any bodies buried under it, but there are carvings; spirals and strange zigzags, powdered with lichen. It seems impossible to me that the Sekoi could have put these up. There are so few Sekoi, and they always seem so lazy.

I didn't spend the night by the thing, but up in the wood, and I wasn't comfortable. Noises whispered among the branches; a faint breeze made the beasts restless, and endless insects plagued me. Once when I sat up and looked down the slope, I had the feeling the stones were looking back. (None of this will go in the report. I don't want to look a fool.)

At first light I set off. The horse-tracks were lost in marsh, but they started to lead west, so that's the way I'll go.

Atelgarsday, evening

I'm writing this in a village called Tis. At least I think that's what they call it. No one here has seen Harn or the boy Raffael, but I've found out one thing—we're not the only ones looking.

A woman here told me that about a week back, a horseman came through. He was asking for a man named Galen Harn, and even knew what he looked like—dark, hook-nosed, a limp.

The Box of Flames

No one could help, and he went off east.

I'm assuming this is a stranger to the Watch, not one of us. So who? It's clear to me he's already found them—the horse-tracks at the cromlech must have been his. A red horse. Painted. They may have gone with him somewhere—if there was word of a relic, the sorcerer would have been drawn to it, undoubtedly.

After careful questioning and a lot of bribes, I've found out the names of a few likely villages, and one nest of bandits. That might be the best bet, as not many villagers have horses. It's west of here, an old Maker-ruin, a lair of thieves. The villagers say the warlord is called Alberic, and if he's the one on our files, then Galen Harn might well be in more trouble than he knows.

And my job might already be done for me.

5

The Wounded City—who can see to the
edge of it?
Who can feel the pain of its loss?

Poems of Anjar Kar

GALEN HESITATED.

Raffi waited without breathing, hating him, desperate for him to give up the box, then not to. He was numb, dizzy with fear.

Galen lowered his aim.

With a snicker of triumph, Alberic loosed his grip on Raffi's hair and held out one small palm. The Relic Master dropped the box into it heavily.

"Thank you." Alberic smirked. "For a moment I thought you wouldn't."

Raffi tugged away across the room, weak with relief. For a moment he had thought the same, and that made him angry. "You should have used it!" he snapped.

"He was too close to you."

"But just to give it to him!"

"Would you rather be dead?" the keeper asked quietly.

"He wanted me as a hostage. He wouldn't have killed me."

"He wanted the box more." Galen glared at him. "We have other weapons, Raffi. Keep your mind on them."

Simmering, Raffi watched Alberic. He had climbed back into his chair and was fingering the box avidly, exploring it by touch. When he looked up his eyes were alert. "So what's wrong with it?"

"Wrong?"

"You wouldn't have given it to me otherwise." He lifted it and pointed it straight at them. Raffi went cold.

"Be careful," Galen said calmly. "It's dangerous."

"That's what I want."

"And unstable. We have no way of knowing how much life is left in it, but it's already hundreds of years old. Maybe very little."

"And maybe a lot." Alberic swung the box and aimed

it at a tall bronze candlestick by the window; Godric and Taran scattered instantly. "Chief!"

"Be quiet." Then he fired.

Light blinded them. When they could see again, the candle was a bubbling, hissing pool of wax and molten metal on the seared floor. There was a shocked silence, and then the tiny man began to laugh. He wheezed and giggled and cackled; jumping from his chair, he cavorted around the candles, catching Sikka's hands and kissing them, then dancing away. His own people watched him in amusement; Raffi stared; Galen stood stiff with distaste.

At last, breathless, Alberic slumped over the arm of his chair, clutching his side. "Oh, this is wonderful!" he managed. "Superb. Beyond belief! To rob a Relic Master!" He lifted the box and rubbed it as gently as if it had been a bird; then his head turned, and his eyes were cold and crafty.

"This is the arrangement. I want the Sekoi. You have power, contacts. You'll find him for me and get him here alive. And then I might, I just might, give you your box of flames back." He stretched over for the wine and took a long drink, then climbed into his chair and sat.

Galen said nothing. His look was dark.

Alberic shrugged. "Think about it. In the meantime you can try my hospitality."

Godric came forward and led them to the door, but just as they got there the sly voice behind them said, "It doesn't sound very inviting, does it? But one thing might interest you, Relic Master. The Sekoi was headed for the city. The city of the Makers. Tasceron."

Galen stood stock-still, as if the word had frozen him. Then, without turning, he stalked out of the room.

ALBERIC'S HOSPITALITY TURNED out to be a locked room, as filthy as the rest of the building, with one threadbare mattress and a window that let in a drizzle of rain and moonlight. Galen sat moodily in a corner, his knees drawn up and his arms resting on them, staring at nothing.

Raffi left him alone. He swept all the filthy straw and dung into one corner with his foot, tossed the mattress after it, then dragged their pack over, and the two plates of food a hand had just banged in through a grille at the base of the door.

He looked them over anxiously. "There's some sort of meat. It looks all right. The bread's stale. Cheese." He tasted the clear liquid in the wooden cup and scowled. "Water. He's not stripping the apple tree for us, is he?"

Galen made a meaningless murmur. Raffi began to eat hurriedly. He was hungry—he was always hungry—and even the stale bread could be moistened with water and broken up. With a few withered shar-roots and herbs from the pack it was almost tasty.

Swallowing a mouthful, he muttered, "So what do we do?"

Galen looked up. In the dim cell his face was haggard. "We agree."

"Just to get out of here? I mean, he'll never give it back."

Galen stirred. He reached into the pack and tugged out the stub of candle, clearing a place in the dust for it. Then he fumbled for the tinderbox.

The blue flame crackled, flared up. When it was steady and yellow, Galen lifted a cup of water and drank thirstily. "Maybe. Maybe not. The spirit of the Makers is in the box. It won't rest with Alberic. It will want to come back to us."

"Then we needn't bother about this Sekoi?"

Galen put down the cup and picked at the food. He had a strange, intent look. "I think I want to bother."

Raffi stopped picking up crumbs with his finger and stared. "You want to run Alberic's errands?"

"My errands."

"But you heard him! We'd have to go to Tasceron!"

Galen smiled then, a wolfish, secret smile. "Sometimes, Raffi, the Makers send their messages through the people you'd least expect. I knew I had to come here; now I know why. I can't hear them any other way, so they speak through Alberic. I knew, as soon as he said it."

Appalled, Raffi ate the rest of the crumbs without tasting anything. Tasceron! Galen was mad.

All his life Raffi had heard about the burning city, the city of the Makers, far to the west. It was vast, a web of a million streets, alleys, bridges, ruins. No one knew half of Tasceron; no one was sure who had built it or when, or what most of the structures were for, the immense marble halls, the squares with their dry fountains. Under the city were said to be tunnels, buried rooms, untold secrets. It was where the palace of the Emperor had been, and the temples of the great relics, and most secret of all, the House of Trees. All lost now, leaving only stories and rumors. The Emperor was dead, the temples destroyed. And the Watch guarded Tasceron, their tall black towers rising among the smoke and stench.

"Suicide," he muttered.

Galen was eating calmly. "No," he said. "I've been thinking of it for some time. In Tasceron something may have survived. Maybe even others of the Order."

Raffi scrambled up and paced about. Then he kicked the wall. "We'd be caught! There must be Watchmen everywhere; how long do you think we'd last? You can't see there, can't even breathe . . ."

Galen looked up sharply. "I'm not mad."

They stared at each other. Slowly, Raffi sat down. "I didn't say that."

"You thought it. You've been thinking it for months. Since the explosion."

Raffi was silent.

Galen gripped his strong fingers together and tapped them against his lips. Then he said steadily, "Since I lost all my power."

There, it was spoken, as it hadn't been spoken in the long summer, since the relic-tube had blown up as Galen was examining it, breaking his leg and his mind, leaving him lying silent for a week, eyes open, unspeaking. He had never said how it felt; Raffi had never dared ask. Now, picking up the empty cup and rolling it in his hands, Raffi knew it was coming.

"For a moment," Galen said, "in that room, I thought Alberic had guessed. But you reassured him." He leaned back against the dim wall, tugging the long hair out of his collar. "I'm empty inside, Raffi. Since the explosion, my mind has been silent. No echoes, no colors, no spirits. I can't move out of myself. I've lost the power and I have to find it again." His voice was raw with pain, with the pent-up agony of months. "I can't . . . exist like this! The trees, the stones, I can't feel them. They speak and I can't hear. Even the relics, the gifts of the Makers themselves—even when I hold those, Raffi, I feel nothing. Nothing!"

Embarrassed, hot with pity that was almost anger, Raffi rocked the cup. He had known this would come out, all Galen's torment. For the last few months the keeper had been a tangle of rage and bewilderment: trying trances, starving himself, storming off into the forest for days, punishing them both with prayers and chants and penances. And never talking about it. Until now.

Because the power was gone. Although he'd only gained a little of it, Raffi guessed the horror of that. The Order had the skills to contact all sorts of life. And in the relics, they touched traces of the Makers themselves, who had come down and lived in the world, built and formed it, and then gone, no one knew where.

It would kill Galen, that loss. Or drive him insane.

"You think there'll be some sort of cure in Tasceron?"

"There must be!" Galen limped around the cell with a pent-up, feverish energy. "There must be some of our people left, someone who could help me! I've got to try anything!"

Crouching, he put his hand on the rocking cup. Raffi looked up; the keeper was watching him, eyes dark. In the candlelight his face was edged with pain, gaunt. "I'm sorry to have to take you into more danger. But I'll need you."

Raffi shrugged. "I made a promise. To go where you go. Into darkness, into light, remember?" Uneasy, he looked away.

THEY SLEPT ON the floor, cold and unbearably hard after the bracken of the forest. For a while Raffi lay awake, listening to the keeper's steady breathing. He knew Galen was desperate. But Tasceron! He'd have to go with him, if only to try and keep them both alive, but he didn't know enough, he was only at the fourth Branch. It wasn't fair, he thought bitterly. And the fires burned under Tasceron, had burned for years. How could any of the Order have survived?

He must have slept, because a long time later someone was shaking him out of unreachable dreams; he groaned and rolled over stiffly. He was soaked with drizzle, the room cold with an early-morning light.

Alberic stood in the doorway, burly men behind him. He wore a silk tunic trimmed with dark fur and small boots that must have cost the shoemaker an immense amount of trouble.

"Mmm." He glanced around the cell. "The guest room could do with a little more work. But then, most of our guests don't leave. What about you?"

Galen stood up, tall and grim. "We've decided. We'll find your Sekoi."

Alberic grinned slyly. "Oh, excellent," he murmured. "I knew you would."

The Bee's Warning

6

The agent must carry out a proper surveillance.

Rule of the Watch

Journal of Carys Arrin
Cyraxday
4.16.546

It was a light of some sort. Nothing like I've ever seen before. Something utterly, brilliantly white, and it flashed out from the top window of the fortress, facing east, two hours after dusk.

If I hadn't been watching the place closely I might have missed it, though both the pack-beast and the horse skittered and stamped in fright. For a moment I was afraid they'd be heard, but I needn't have worried; all the animals in Alberic's pens were just as terrified; the clamor of geese and the barking of all the dogs came up clear through the drizzle.

I got to the fortress this afternoon, and camped on a rocky knoll above it. It's sheltered here. Two great pines sprout out over the cliff; by climbing one I'm well hidden and have a good view of Alberic's defenses. (A separate report on these will go to the Watch as soon as I find someone to take it.)

At first there were a lot of people about; as it got dark and the weather closed in, they went indoors. A fine, gray drizzle fell, but I was well sheltered. After the light flashed out, I lay along the branch and thought about it. First, it had to mean that Galen Harn was inside the fortress. Only he could have done that, or his scholar— though according to our information Raffael Morel has only been with him for four years, since Harn took him from his father's farm.

And they must have used a relic. This was no wood and water mumbo jumbo, no sacred trees or spirit journeys. This was something brimming with power, blinding. Something of the Makers.

For a long time I waited, fidgeting with curiosity. What was going on in there? Harn and Alberic must be in some plot together, brewing something against the Watch. If only I could have gotten inside!

Ten minutes later, the light came again.

The Bee's Warning

I was ready this time, and it may have been nearer the window, or simply stronger, because the ray was breathtaking—pure white, so that in one instant I saw all the roofs of the buildings below lit in a sudden stark glare; squalid walls and rain and a pig lying on its side in a sty. Then blackness.

It seemed to shock the people of the fortress just as much—they came running out of all the doors and clustered, staring up.

Nothing else, all night. I ate cold food and put the beasts in shelter, then lay on the branch and watched. Three moons shone on the thieves' tower—even in the dappled moonlight the pale walls gleamed. Whoever the Makers were, they could build. An owl is hooting in the wood; the wet branches stir around me, dripping on this page.

Tomorrow, if nothing else happens, I'll have to try and get inside. This might not be too difficult. My face isn't known—after all, this is my first real mission, first time outside the Watchhouse. And according to what I've heard, Alberic's tower is a nest of cutthroats, poachers, thieves, renegades. People come and go there all the time, with no real rules except Alberic's orders. Maybe no one will notice one more vagabond.

Especially if she is a girl.

Karnosday, early

No need. They're coming out. Two figures have just left the gate, and they look like Harn and the boy. They must be in some plot with Alberic—he'd never let them go otherwise. It'll take me a while to get down the hill and after them. But this is luck, real luck.

Dead or alive, say the orders. And I won't lose them now.

7

The Order will survive. They can never kill us all. Underground, well hidden, we have knowledge that can outlive the world.

Reputed last words of Mardoc Archkeeper, from the rack

"ARE YOU SURE?" Galen stood on the grass under the oak and stared back at the misty country they had crossed.

"Not sure." Raffi shrugged, uneasy. "Just a feeling. As if someone touched me and drew back. It may have been nothing."

"Unlikely." Galen hadn't moved; shading his eyes from the rising sun, he stared east. "It could have been an animal."

"Do you think Alberic is having us followed?"

Galen came and sat on the wet grass. "I doubt that."

"But he knows we could go anywhere!"

79

"He has the box."

"Yes, and that was a big mistake."

Galen gave him an icy glare. "If I want your opinion, boy, I'll ask. The box is nearly dead. And he's greedy but wily. He'll keep it for himself, a personal weapon to keep his rabble in order. He won't risk wasting it."

Raffi simmered, his back against the ridged oak bark. Galen was right. He was always right. Except about Tasceron.

"Well," the Relic Master said grimly, "if you think someone's following, you'd better look back." He looked resentful. "Take your time."

Raffi sat back, tried to relax, breathed in the cold damp. Under his palms he felt the crushed stalks of grass. Slowly, his third eye opened. He looked back along the paths of the last day and night, felt the stir of small animals along the hedgerows, the giant ant-castle where the track crossed the stream. He tasted the dreams of the sleepers in the village they had skirted, smelled the great silent strength of the trees, the leaf-rot, the strange nightwalkers among them. Along the waterlines he went, and the earth tracks, back, far back, as far as he could reach, and all he felt at the edge of the land was the sun, a red heat, a blaze that rose with a searing pain out of the steams of the valley.

His lips opened; no words came.

Galen grabbed his arm. "Stop it. You're burning."

Raffi dragged himself back, such a long way. Opening his eyes, he felt drained; he was sweating, dizzy.

"Don't look into the sun!" Galen was angry. "How many times have I told you that! Was there anyone?"

"I don't know," Raffi said faintly.

Galen stood up and limped around. "If only I could see!" he cried, raging, banging down his stick.

"Don't shout," Raffi moaned.

Galen glared at him, then nudged the pack with his foot. "Drink something. It helps."

Feeling a failure, Raffi got the water out and drank thirstily. It ran down his chin; he dragged the cool drops over his hot face. He was tired and wished they would stop; it was dangerous to travel in the day.

A few minutes later Galen came and stood over him. "Not your fault," he said gruffly. "Not enough practice."

"Not your fault either," Raffi said quietly.

The keeper jabbed the turf with his stick. "Isn't it?" He looked up, out ahead. "Come on. Let's find somewhere to lay low."

IT WAS STILL EARLY, and the fields were waist-deep in damp mist. Walking through them seemed more like wading; browsing flocks of tiny birds rose up in clouds before them. This was someone's pasture, lush and green, the hedgerows thick with leaves and bines, the trees already losing their leaves. A herd of tawny cattle wandered in the fields beyond, staring, chewing, at the passing strangers.

Raffi chewed back at them. It was easy country to walk, low and firm underfoot. Lanes and small tracks crisscrossed it; gates were in good repair. It was a different world to the forest. But the people also made it dangerous.

Climbing down a hedge bank into a deep hollow lane, he saw that Galen had stopped. The Relic Master stood tall among the white flowers of the hedge, the pack on his back, listening. Then he turned. "Anything?"

The Bee's Warning

"Someone ahead. Near."

As Raffi said it, she came around the corner of the lane: a large woman, wrapped in rough shawls, avoiding the puddles. She carried a small sack in her arms; it seemed heavy as she put it down and straightened wearily. Then she saw them.

"Be careful," Galen whispered.

"You don't need to tell me that!"

There was no way of avoiding her. The lane was deep, the hedges high on each side, spiny and tangled. They walked on quickly, Galen's staff sticking in the soft ground.

The woman waited, hands on hips. She probably had some weapon, Raffi thought. He put his head down and tried to look pitiable. As he was wet through and tired, that was easy.

"Fine day," Galen said quietly as they came up to her.

The woman nodded; she looked at them both with a shrewd interest. "For traveling, it is. Have you come by the village?"

"A different way." Galen rubbed his chin with the back of one hand, then he stopped, digging the stick in and leaning both hands on it. His long strings of black jet and green crystals swung in the pale light. "Can you tell me about the pathways hereabouts?"

She didn't seem afraid. "I could. Where are you going?"

He hesitated. "The coast."

"It's four days' walk." She turned slightly, but still watched them both. "You should keep heading west. Make for that stone on the ridge up there." She pointed, and far off Raffi saw a tiny pillar on the skyline, dark against the clouds. "From there the track goes on, clear over the chalklands. Lots of old tombs up there—Sekoi country. I wouldn't pass it at night." She scratched her neck. "But you may not mind."

If that was a hint, Galen ignored it. "Where do we cross the river?" he asked.

She laughed shortly, then looked at him carefully. "Well upstream. Almost at the top of the valley. Half a day's tramp."

"Isn't there a nearer ford? Or a bridge?"

For a moment she said nothing. Then, strangely, "Oh, there's a bridge, master. At the bottom of the gully. But no

The Bee's Warning

one can cross it. Take my advice and keep away from it."

Raffi felt Galen's interest. "Why?"

Instead of answering, she said, "We all fear the Watch, stranger, don't we?"

"Indeed we do," Galen said very quietly.

"Then listen. The bridge is a thing of the Makers. Many have tried to cross it and can't, that's all I know. Go upstream." Then she almost smiled. "I see I'm wasting my advice."

Galen looked at her steadily. "Thank you."

"Take care. If you were one of the old Order I might ask for your blessing."

"If I were one of the old Order I would give it."

She nodded briefly, then picked up her sack and trudged past Raffi. He moved aside for her; saw her glance at him, sharp and interested. She knew who they were. But none of them would say anything, just in case.

At the end of the track she turned. "Keep that boy of yours fed," she called. "He looks half starved."

Then she was gone, brushing through the wet sprays of hawthorn, so that the drops fell in a glinting shower.

Raffi glanced at Galen. "So."

Galen tugged his stick out of the mud. "Let's go and see this bridge."

Raffi sighed. "I knew we would."

At the end of the track was a field path, and then a tiny stone-lined gully, leading down to the left between dripping trees. The going was steep; the wet stones slippery and so overgrown that Galen had to slash away the weeds.

"Not many use this," Raffi gasped, slipping.

"They did once." Galen snapped a branch with an effort, muttering the prayer that would calm the tree. "It's cobbled. That was done for a reason."

As they went down, Raffi felt the age of the rutted way. It became a green tunnel of leaves; great ferns and banks of cowflax and horsetails, meadowsweet and tiny carpets of purple flowers that climbed and sprouted between the stones.

Crouching, pushing the wet leaves aside, he found that both sides of the track were walled; Galen was right, it had once been important. But now it was dim and dripping with rain from the trees overhead, so that small runnels of water slid down through the red mud and over the stones where Raffi's feet slithered and splashed.

Down they went, into the valley's depths. The air became sticky, clammy with pollen; small flies droned in the clumps of white umbrels, their sweet stench pungent. Below him, Galen was flecked with light, gold tints of sunlight on his back as he passed through a brighter patch. "Coming out," he muttered.

Raffi scrambled down, one ankle aching. At the bottom, balanced on two stones with the water trickling between, he turned and looked back up the green hollow. It dripped silently. If anyone was following, he'd have to come down the same way. For a moment he thought, then crouched to the stone under his boot and, putting a finger in the wet mud, drew a design carefully on it. A black bee, gatherer and storer—one of the signs of the Order. He threw a handful of clotted leaves to cover it. Now we'll see, he thought.

The hollow widened onto the riverbank, a steep incline of red mud, the exposed roots of great beech trees sprawled over it like a natural stairway. Galen was already climbing down. Beyond him, Raffi saw the bridge.

It was a bizarre structure. Low, only inches above the

water, and made of chains; black, seemingly wooden chains that had splintered and split in places. Planks hung from them, looking half rotten. On the two heavy posts rammed into the shore were carvings—faces, grotesque and snarling—and a few snags of cloth and feathers hung from poles nearby.

Jumping down, Raffi stood by Galen. "People are still afraid of it."

"I'm not surprised."

The river was sluggish and choked with weeds and sedges; mist hung over it, so that the bridge led into gray uncertainty. Thick green weed trailed under the surface like hair.

Raffi swiped at mosquitoes. "It's becoming a swamp."

"What about the bridge?" Galen asked coldly.

Sighing, Raffi tried to sense it, but it was just mist and drift, and he was tired. "Can't we sleep?" he muttered. "The sun's up, we've been walking all night. No one's likely to come here."

"We stop when I say!" Galen shrugged the pack off and threw his stick on it. He walked to the bridge and put a hand on each of the black posts and stood there

The Bee's Warning

a moment, looking into the mist. Raffi knew he was straining to feel something. Anything. When he spoke, the keeper's voice was harsh with defeat.

"I'm crossing. Stay here. If I call you, come."

"Look." Raffi hesitated. "Shouldn't I . . . ?"

"No! I'm still the Master."

Galen edged forward cautiously. The black chains tightened; the bridge creaked and swung, but it seemed strong enough to hold him. He walked on, step by step, avoiding the broken planks, merging into the mist that rose from the stagnant water. Slowly it closed around him, and he was gone.

Raffi waited, anxious. The river rippled quietly, stinking of rot. A snake slithered between reeds and flicked away. Nothing else moved. The silence was intense, suddenly eerie. Raffi came to the end of the bridge and gripped the posts. "Galen?"

Before he could call again he caught a movement in the mist. Galen's dark figure loomed out of it, walking carefully. When he looked up, he seemed astonished.

He stared at Raffi strangely. Then he stepped off the bridge and stood in the mud. He looked around.

"What happened?" Raffi demanded. "Why did you come back?"

"See for yourself."

"What?"

Galen sat on the bank. He seemed bewildered and amused about it. "Go on. Take a look."

Raffi stared, then turned abruptly and walked out onto the bridge. He went quickly, jumping the splintered boards, avoiding the gaps in the rail. When he looked back, the bank was lost in mist. Mist drifted all around him; a waterbird croaked in it.

Ahead of him, as the bridge swayed, he saw something. Trees on a bank, beech trees, high and green. One plank went soft underfoot; he stepped over it quickly and looked up. The bank loomed out of grayness.

Raffi stopped dead in astonishment.

Galen was sitting by the pack, legs stretched out. He waved a long hand. "So," he said sarcastically. "What happened? Why did you come back?"

"I didn't! I went straight across!"

The keeper laughed grimly. "So did I, Raffi. So did I."

8

"Now," Flain said, "we must have a messenger to go between us and God."

The eagle said, "Let it be me." But the eagle was too proud.

The bee-bird said, "Let it be me." But the bee-bird was too vain.

The crow said, "Let it be me. I'm dark, an eater of carrion. I have nothing to be proud of."

So Flain chose the crow, and whispered the secrets to it.

Book of the Seven Moons

IT WAS AMAZING. And infuriating. Three times now,
Raffi had crossed the bridge. Each time he came back to
where he'd started from.

"It's impossible," he muttered. "I mean, it's not circular, it doesn't turn! I don't understand!"

Galen sat on the bank, legs crossed. He had pulled
some orange fungi from the bole of a dead tree; now he
was frying them in the small pan over a carefully smoke-
less fire.

"What have I taught you?" he said. "Understanding's
not enough. Understanding is from outside; merely a
function of the mind."

Raffi sighed. "I know."

"To enter, that's the secret. To become the bridge, to crawl into its sap, to sway with it, to rot over centuries as its heartwood rots. When you are the bridge you will know what the bridge knows. It takes time. A lifetime. And skill."

Sullenly, Raffi sat down. Galen gave him a sharp glance.

"You know it but you don't apply it. You're lazy. Now think. How could the bridge be like this?"

Raffi was scowling at the sizzling mushrooms, counting the pieces. He said, "It could be a device of the Makers. Though it doesn't look that old."

Galen nodded, shaking the pan. Pig fat spat and crackled. "Possible. The entire bridge a relic. It could be older than it seems. The wood is from no tree I know. What else?"

Raffi swallowed. "Aren't they ready yet?"

"Concentrate. What else?"

He forced himself to think. "A protection spell. Someone who lives on the other side."

"Also possible. Here, take some now."

Raffi jabbed his knife in and dragged out one slice carefully, waving it, eating it before it cooled so that it burned his mouth. He gulped down three more without speaking, then paused, with another on his knife.

"What about the Sekoi?"

"No." Galen chewed slowly. "Not this. I have a feeling this is one of ours."

"Ours."

"The Order."

Raffi sat up. "Someone alive?"

"Maybe." Galen stared at the bridge, his eyes deep and dark. "There were men in the Order once with great skills, boy. They knew the mightiest relics—handled them every day. The power of the Makers lingered in them. They knew strange things—things that have never been written, maybe even the secrets of the Makers themselves. An old man once told me that when the Makers departed the world, they left behind a certain book of their deeds wrapped in black cloth. Only one man knew the script it was written in. The knowledge was taught, from one Archkeeper to the next, till Mardoc was betrayed. Maybe someone still knows it."

He stood up abruptly, emptied the fat from the pan,

and swirled it in the river, leaving a greasy trail. Then he tossed the pan down next to Raffi. "Pack up. You can carry it."

"But where?"

"Over the bridge, where else?" Galen dragged his stick up and gave a sudden, sidelong grimace. "I may have lost my powers, but I still have my memory. Words may be enough, if you know the right ones."

At the bridge end he took some red mud and crouched, making two images on the carved posts, waving Raffi back so he couldn't see what they were. Then he pushed the tangled nettles back over them. Sucking the edge of one hand, he stood up.

Raffi watched. A tingle of excitement stirred in him. Already he could sense something new; it leaked from the hidden signs like a faint aroma.

Galen stood on the bridge and began to murmur. It was an old prayer, one Raffi had heard only once before, littered with the ancient half-understood words of the Makers. The keeper's deep voice hoarsened as he spoke them; the air lightened, as if something in the mist curled up, retreated. Raffi came forward quickly.

The Bee's Warning

Galen fell silent, listening. "Well?"

"It feels as though something's changed."

"Then I was right. Stay near." They stepped out onto the bridge; it slipped and swayed under them. Mist swirled over the sedges; Raffi gripped the worn wooden chains, feeling the whole shaky contraption rattle under him. But this time it was different. As they crossed he saw trees loom out of the damp, not beeches but oaks—old, squat, hollow trees—and holly, and thorn, crowding right to the bank.

"You did it!"

Galen nodded. He stopped at the rotting end of the bridge and looked around. "But this isn't the other bank. It seems to be some sort of island in the river. Tiny. And overgrown. No one's been here for years."

The disappointment was hard in his voice.

Crushing foxglove and bracken, they pushed their way in. The island had a silence that made Raffi uneasy. No birds sang. Above the gnarled branches the sky was blue, pale as eggshell. He realized the morning was half over.

Galen stopped. Before them was a house, or it had been, once. Now only a few fragments of wall rose among a thicket of elder; red wall, made of mud brick. A single window with a black shutter hung open. Trampling down nettles, Raffi clambered up and looked inside.

The room was a grove of trees. Oaks had splintered it; over the years its outline had faded under ivy, swathes of fungus on rotting wood. Half a chimney still rose up, weeds waving from its top.

A crash made him jump; Galen had forced his way in, through a cloud of seed and gnats.

Raffi followed. "Was it ours?"

"I should think so."

"But why the protection spell? There's nothing here to protect."

Galen threw him a scornful look. "That's what we're meant to think. Go and get the pack."

When he'd dragged it in, he found Galen kneeling at the hearth, brushing earth and worms from flat red bricks that were smashed and broken. The keeper eased his filthy nails in and forced one up; it moved with a strange hoarse gasp.

The earth underneath was smooth. Galen tugged the next stone out.

The Bee's Warning

"What are you looking for?"

"Anything. The spell was strong. Something's here worth guarding."

"Relics!"

"Almost certainly." Another tile came out and left a dark gap. Raffi crouched down quickly. He had felt the shock of power, faint but unmistakable. "Something's in there!"

Galen widened the hole, reached in, and seemed to scrabble and dig with his fingers. He paused, then he pulled his hands out in a shower of soil.

He was holding a small packet, wrapped in layers of waxed cloth. Shuffling back, he turned and carefully laid it on a flat stone.

"Is it dangerous?" he asked without looking up.

"I don't think so." Raffi felt inadequate, the old feeling. "I don't really know."

Galen shot him a glance. Then he unwrapped the packet, his fingers working eagerly. Raffi knew he was taking a chance.

The cloth opened. They saw a small glass ball, and a piece of rough parchment made from some thin bark.

This had rotted and, even as Galen opened it, infinitely carefully, pieces flaked off. Then it split, and he hissed with frustration.

The writing was faint, barely a scrawl, and some words had gone. Galen read it out grimly.

Kelnar, of the Order of keepers. To any others of the Sacred Way who still live and . . . come this way. The Watch . . . from the chalk hills. The Archkeeper Tesk died yesterday, they took him. They know I'm here, I have to go to find . . . I have little time. Understand this. I have seen the Crow. The Crow still lives in the dark places of Tasceron, in the House of Trees, deep underground, guarded with spells. I cannot say. . . .

Galen frowned. "This bit's very broken. I can just get words: *hollow, sacred, the messenger.* Then, *Find him. Find him. Prayers and blessings, brothers. Strength of the rock, cunning of the weasel be yours.*"

He looked up. "That's all."

Carefully, he sifted the tiny scraps that had fallen, trying to find more.

"The Crow!" Raffi breathed the words in awe. "Still alive!"

The Bee's Warning

"Tesk died twenty years ago. That dates it."

But Raffi could see the news had shaken Galen, stirred him deep. He wanted to ask more, about what it meant, but instead he picked up the ball carefully. It was cold, heavy, quite transparent. He turned it in his fingers. Nothing came from it now. It was silent.

Galen took it from him. "A relic. But of what?" He muttered a prayer over it, a brief blessing. "Once I saw an image of the Crow carrying such a glass ball in his mouth. A most secret sign. But what it means, I never learned."

"Did you know him?" Raffi asked.

"Kelnar? No. Not even the name. But the Order was great when I was a scholar. There were hundreds of keepers."

"I wonder what happened to him."

Galen scowled. He wrapped the ball back in the waxed cloth and, picking the letter up, read it again. Then he crushed it in his strong grip. Fragments of desiccated parchment gusted in the river breeze.

"Dead," he said softly. "Like all of them."

THEY DECIDED TO SLEEP on the island. With the spell on the bridge, and on the second bridge that led through a great bank of nettles to the far shore, there was nowhere safer. Raffi was too tired to think about what they had found. He drank hot tea made of nettle leaves and curled up hastily in a blanket in the shelter of the ruined wall.

His dreams were strange. He found himself walking endlessly over a grassy plain; a great city lay before him, its spires and towers rising over the horizon, but he could never reach it, never get any closer. And behind him his shadow stretched, long and black, and it danced and capered with glee, he knew it did, but every time he turned and looked at it, it kept still. Walking on, he felt the evil dance break out again behind him. There was nothing he could do about it.

When he woke, he lay with his eyes closed, sleepily, trying to remember. Dreams were important. Perhaps someone was following them. The Watch, he thought, in sudden terror. Or Alberic. But whoever it was, the bridge would stop him. Relieved, he knew that was true. No one else could cross that.

The Bee's Warning

When he sat up, the sky was dim—the sun had set into red streaks toward the west. Cloud was building there, a sullen bank of weather; gnats and humflies gathered in twisting columns among the sedges.

He made the fire, boiled water, found some roots and a solitary duck's egg. When Galen woke they said the long chant of the day solemnly, sitting under a willow, their hands spread. Then they ate. Galen halved the egg, though it was his by right. Spitting out some shell, he said, "We'll stay here tonight and go on in the morning. It'll be more dangerous, but we shouldn't cross the burial hills at night."

"Good," Raffi muttered, his mouth full.

Galen sat back, folding his arms. Then he said, "Who is the Crow, Raffi?"

Raffi swallowed hastily. But he knew the ritual; the Litany of the Makers had always fascinated him.

"The Crow is the messenger. In the beginning the Crow flew between the Makers and God. He carried their words, written in gold letters. He spoke their words to God. Later, when the Makers left Anara and went to the seven sisters in the heavens, the Crow brought messages from them to the keepers and Relic Masters of the Order."

"Is the Crow a bird?"

"The Crow is a bird and not a bird. He is a man and not a man."

"Is the Crow a voice?"

"He is the voice of the Makers."

Galen nodded. "Good. I've neglected the Litany with you lately."

"Knowing the answers is one thing," Raffi said. "I'm still not sure what they mean."

Galen stirred the fire and laughed harshly. "Wise men have spent their lives on them. A four-year scholar knows nothing yet. The Crow is a spiritual being. He can take many forms. He's real."

"Have you ever . . . seen him?"

Galen looked up, surprised. Then he shrugged. "I was no older than you when the Order was destroyed. Such visions were far above me. What I've learned since then has been from Malik, my own master, from the Book, from the few of the Order I've met. The great visions are shattered, Raffi. Our knowledge is in pieces, in the ashes of burned libraries. Only in Tasceron might there be someone who knows the answers."

Raffi looked up at the moons; Atterix and Pyra, almost together. "The man who wrote that letter—he says he saw the Crow."

"A lot can happen in twenty years." Galen's eyes were shadows, but as he shifted, Raffi saw them glint strangely. "And yet the Crow is immortal. If we could find him, speak to him . . . If he could take our message to the Makers . . . If the Makers would come back . . ."

He was silent, choked with the joy of it, and Raffi too, hearing the ripple of the sluggish water, the splash of a bird settling for the night. Then, with a hiss of pain he snatched his hand up.

Galen looked over. "What's wrong?"

"A bee sting!"

A small red lump was swelling on his wrist. He put it to his mouth, sucking at the pain.

"At night?"

Raffi let the throb subside. Then he said, "It's not a real bee. I put the sign of the bee on a stone at the bottom of that track we came down. Someone just stood on it."

9

The Watch is unsleeping. Never relent in the search; never turn back.

Rule of the Watch

Journal of Carys Arrin
Larsnight
7.16.546

I've lost them.

And this is so infuriating I can hardly get the words down, but what stopped me was a spell.

There's no other word for it. Every time I tried to cross that bridge I found myself back where I started! It seems to be some sort of power field to confuse the mind—I can't believe that it actually changes matter in any way or that the bridge can have only one end. In all my training, the Watchleaders insisted that the powers of the Order were an illusion—I can see fat old Jeltok now, banging his cane on the table. Well, it's an illusion that's worked on me.

Galen Harn had crossed. I found traces of a

campfire on the bank and scraps of food—fungus of some sort. Maybe they brew a concoction of this and drink it to counteract the spell. Too risky to try without knowing more.

In the end I had to give up. Even leading the horse into the swamp would have been useless—the whole area was thick with seedbeds and alder; soft, probably deep. I almost screamed with frustration, and kicked the black rotting chains of the thing with hatred.

What makes it worse is that they're traveling by night. Harn is cunning. He's been hunted all his life; he knows how to blend with the leaves and the land, though I don't believe that non-sense that the keepers can turn into trees and stones.

It was well after dark when I turned back from the bridge and though I'd slept a little, I was tired. Yesterday I sold the pack-beast and most of the goods in a village beyond the fields—speed is more important now. But I kept the horse, and that's one advantage. They're on foot.

I rode the horse back up the stony gully and turned east, quickly crossing the fields in the

The Bee's Warning

dark. My plan was to follow the river upstream until I could cross it. The wind was chill and the stubbly ground uneven; worst of all it rose constantly, and the river ran below in a steep cleft with ash and elder springing out of the sides. There was no way down—I just had to keep going, farther away from the bridge all the time.

Furious, I strapped my jerkin tight and kicked the horse on; we galloped now, leaping small walls and hedges, four moons watching us through cloud. Down lanes bordered with stone walls, past a dark farmhouse, skirting tangled copses; the search for a track seemed endless. It was almost light before I found it. A narrow, beaten trail. It looked as if animals had trodden it; it led into a dark stand of juniper and fireberry bushes, and smelled of night-cat.

The horse didn't like it. Neither did I, I suppose, but time was pressing and I was angry and a bit reckless. So I rode down. I can see old Jellie shaking his head now.

It was dark among the trees, the branches low and tangled. I had to dismount, slashing them aside, leading the horse. Uneasy, fly-bitten, and scratched, we scrambled down, tread muffled on a springy mattress of needles, the winter's shriveled berries. The track dropped steeply and the horse kept whickering, the smell of its fear sharp on the air. I swore at it, then swung my crossbow out and racked it hastily. In the undergrowth a twig had cracked.

I stopped, raising the bow. The copse was dim. Ahead, somewhere below, I could see a pale daylight, but here the trunks crowded, silent.

I heard it before it leaped and squirmed around; the yowl was in my face, past me, then the lithe black shape had fastened onto the horse; it reared, screaming with terror. I aimed too fast; the bolt shot wide, crunched in an ash-bole. Then the horse was gone, in a heedless bloodstained panic, the night-cat streaking after it like a shadow.

Furious, I scrambled down the track, all hope gone. I'd seen what a night-cat could do—there'd be no chance of riding back to the bridge. And I was scared, believe me. But I needed the food and money in the saddlebags. Everything was on that wretched horse. Then as I came out of the trees, I fell smack over something lying in the path, and stared at it, on hands and knees.

The Bee's Warning

The night-cat lay sprawled, mid-jump. One paw was flung up, the snarling mouth wide in the agony of its death. It was still hot. Fleas jumped off it. I reached out cautiously and touched it. The great head slumped; blood clotted the black fur, just congealing. A crossbow bolt stuck out of its neck.

I rolled under the nearest bush, racked the bow hastily, and reloaded it. I'd missed the cat. This was someone else's work. And they'd be back for it. Steadying my breath, controlling, I waited for them under the leaves. Always see what you're up against, Jellie used to wheeze. I'd never believed he'd been a field agent, not then, but his captures were listed in all the Watchtowers, so he must have been thinner once.

Two minutes later a blackbird screeched and flew off. I heard voices coming up the path from the river. Putting my eye to the sight of the bow I watched them come, two men, shouldering through bracken, my sweating, nervous horse dragging behind.

I could have killed them both. Or maybe one; the other would have gone before I could reload, and then it would have been cat and mouse, and I had no idea who else might be around. Safer to wait.

They stood over the cat, laughing, more than pleased with themselves. The bigger one gazed up the track. "The rider might still be alive."

"Maybe."

"Should we look?"

The smaller one laughed and shook his head. "Not me. Cat's had him. Or he broke his neck coming off. This horse is worth at least fifty marks, never mind the stuff in the bags."

"What if he turns up?"

They looked at each other. Then they laughed again.

I had to take my finger off the trigger, force myself to be calm. I get angry too easily, and an agent needs control. They didn't know I was Watch. I could have gotten up and told them— they might have backed off. Or might not. Bitterly I lay where I was, deep in leaves, woodbugs crawling over me. And all the time Galen Harn was slipping away.

They were in no hurry. They skinned the cat on the spot, taking the soft thick pelt, the teeth,

114

the paws, some of the innards. Soon the air stank of blood; flies buzzed in clouds over the carcass. Finally, well into the morning, they gathered up their packs, loaded them onto the horse, and set off, down toward the river. They talked loud and easy, but their bows were ready.

Stiff and filthy, I watched them go, then got up and followed, silent, from bush to tree. I may not be one of the magical Order, but even as kids in the Watchhouses, we played this game. No one caught me then. Or now.

It took over an hour to reach the farm. I smelled it first, the tang of cattle over the marshy ground; then I saw the low rise of the roof, close to the water. The river was narrower here, still sluggish but shallow; I could see cows knee-deep in it on a bank of shingle. I could have crossed. But I wanted the horse.

The men tied it up and went inside.

Flat behind low scrub, I looked the place over. Not a village, as I'd feared, but a house, isolated. Maybe fewer than ten people. Abruptly the door opened; the two men were back, women with them, an old man, children. They fed the horse an apple, walked around it, slapped its legs admiringly. A small girl in a tattered dress was lifted onto its back.

There were dogs, of course. Two. I was downwind, which was just as well, but they terrified me. Dogs you can never trust. Then I saw the saddlebags were open. Bit by bit, my food supplies went into the house. I saw them holding up my clothes, surprised, and managed a sour laugh. I was small, even for a girl. What were they thinking now?

Finally, when I'd almost wriggled away and given up, they all went in. I slid forward quickly, through the marshy tussocks. Frustration broke out—suddenly I was reckless and fierce. I'd lost so much time; if I was to act it had to be now, before they came back!

With the thought I was up, running, head bent low, into the muddy yard. The horse whinnied; I slashed the rope and was on its back kicking my heels in hard; we were halfway through the gate when the shouts erupted. I didn't look back but drove the beast hard, mud splashing high, cows scattering. Barking and yells and the whistle of a shot smacked from somewhere, but we were slithering down the

The Bee's Warning

red bank into the water; I shouted and kicked anxiously.

The river was sluggish; boulders choked the peat-brown water, the shingle underneath soft and treacherous. The horse sank in it; a splash and a bark behind warned me, and turning I saw a dog close, its white teeth snapping at the horse's tail.

That probably helped. The horse kicked. Then its hooves grounded in firm soil; I felt it and whooped with delight as we raced over the grass and into the tree cover beyond, a steady joyous run with the wet mane flicking drops into my face like diamonds. Defiant, I sat up. Another bolt splintered bark a meter to my left, but by then I was too reckless to care, and in seconds the trees were around us, and I had to slow the horse.

It took me an hour to calm down.

When I did, I was tired and hungry, and suddenly cold. The wood had petered out; I found myself climbing the slopes of a high bare landscape of chalk, the turf cropped low, and the huge sun in a furnace of gathering cloud. Rain began, drizzling lightly. There was nothing to eat, and no shelter.

Coming carefully over the skyline, I sat still, watching the clouds gather. The empty country stretched out below; dark, smooth green slopes. Pulling the bags off, I let the horse rest, pulled out this book, and wrote. I'm lucky to still have it.

Harn must be far from here by now. He must be out in the middle of these downlands, somewhere. I sit silent, writing, and the horse crops the grass. The tearing of the stalks is loud in the drizzle.

10

Flain the Tall built a tower, and he
called it the House of Trees. This was
because the trees gave their wood for it
freely, without pain. All the trees of the
wood offered a branch, and the House
was fragrant with calarna and yew
and oak, pale willow, red hazel, dark
mahogany.

"This," he said, "will be the court
of the Makers; without guile, without
hardship."

And the battlements were living
branches, woven tight in a web.

Book of the Seven Moons

"WHAT ARE THEY?" Raffi whispered.

"Burial places." Galen didn't turn. He was staring out at the strange country before them, the short grass, the hard white stony track that led away so clearly they could see it mount the ridge and vanish over the top. The sky was immense, Raffi thought, pale blue, as if he could brush it with his hand.

"But are they safe?"

Galen glared at him. "Don't fear the dead. They're not our enemies." Carefully he poured the last drop of red wine into the cleared circle of chalk; it sank into the dry rubble, as if the ground was thirsty, and the small ring of

121

pebbles seemed charged for an instant with clarity. Far ahead the green downs brightened.

They had stayed on the island a day and a night, resting. Nowhere else was safer and, despite Galen's restlessness, he knew they'd needed it. Raffi had fished, mostly. Galen had eaten little and then gone off on his own, and hours later Raffi had come across him sitting in the ruined house, deep in trance, his fingers moving over the black and green awen-beads.

Uneasy, Raffi had retreated to the fire and eaten the rest of the fish. He knew Galen like this. He just had to wait, sleeping on and off, sitting up to stare anxiously into the dark.

At last, late on the second night, the keeper had stumbled through the nettles, thrown himself down, and slept. Raffi sat up and looked at him. He was exhausted, soaked with sweat. Tugging the blanket over him, Raffi curled up in his own worry. Galen was killing himself. The constant struggle, the useless desperate search for his lost power was driving him to madness. They had to get some help! And with Galen's magic gone, all their defenses against the Watch had dwindled to his own sense-lines, frailer the farther he sent them.

Rubbing the bee sting, he wondered what more he could do. Someone had followed them down that path. That overgrown, unused path.

NOW, HIGH ON THE DOWNS, he thought of it again. "I don't like traveling in daylight."

"Maybe, but the woman is right. Here, daylight is best." Galen had shouldered the pack, his long hair tied back in a knot of string. "Keep the lines out."

"You don't have to tell me that!"

Abruptly Galen caught up his stick; Raffi jerked back but the Relic Master gave a sour laugh. "Come on."

They walked all morning, quickly, not speaking. The track climbed the smooth slopes easily, the grass green and short, spattered with rabbit dung. Distant flocks of fat sheep grazed.

On the top of the ridge they lay low, till Galen was sure no one was near; they crept over, not straightening till they were well below the skyline. The stone they had

seen from the valley leaned beside the white track, glinting with quartz.

"Sekoi," Raffi said, seeing the carved spirals.

Galen grunted, walked around it. Then he touched it,
feeling for the bands of energy, but Raffi knew by the way
he turned away that he had failed.

"What's that?"

It was a small red flower, lying propped against the
stone. Galen picked it up. "Not from here. It's been
brought."

"Alberic's Sekoi! He's come past here—and not too
long ago. It's still fresh."

Galen nodded, then tossed it down. "Then I hope the
creature puts on speed. I want Tasceron, not him."

It was a bare place, green to the world's end, and the
sky blue and empty. Trudging, Raffi felt exposed, open to
attack, and through the eyes of the one circling hawk high
up he managed to see himself briefly, a tiny dusty figure,
hot and tired and thirsty, moving with infinite slowness
over the green hollows. The bird swooped and swerved;
giddily he came back to himself, stumbling over a stone.

Then they came to the tombs. A few loomed up, huge,

on each side of the track, smooth humps of grass, some with ditches around them, one with a rowan tree sprouting from the top. For each Galen spoke prayers, chanting under his breath, mile after mile. It was a dry country, incredibly still, with only a sudden arrowbird darting up to break the crisp silence.

Raffi trudged on. The tombs oppressed him; their silence was a weight on his shoulders. He wondered if Galen felt it. Unlike the cromlech, these kept their dead, and passing one he saw for a moment the hidden dark chamber under the grass, the scrawled spirals on the long bones.

Ahead, a ridge rose up. To the left of it a single tree-clump stood, dark tops moving in the breeze. Rooks flapped and cawed above it, a black, restless colony.

Galen stopped. He looked up at the trees, his face stern. Then he stepped off the track. "This way."

Raffi stared. "Why over there?"

"Where I go, you go." He hadn't slowed. Raffi had to hurry to catch him.

"But why?"

"Because I say so."

"That's not enough. It's not enough!" Suddenly angry, Raffi grabbed his sleeve and forced him around. Galen stared at him, eyes black. Raffi forced himself not to step back. Then he said, "I have to look after us both. I have to read the signs, as well as I can. You can't do it. You wouldn't know, if anything was wrong." He let go of the keeper's sleeve and said quietly, "You have to let me warn you, Galen."

Galen didn't move. It was the truth, but Raffi knew he felt it like a blow to the face.

"So what is wrong?" he growled.

"The tombs. They're watching us."

"And the tree?"

He shrugged. "It feels strange."

Galen stabbed the ground with his stick. Then he said, "Listen. Yesterday, I had a dream. The only dream I've had for months. Faintly, in all the pain and the darkness, I saw this place. Those trees up there. Nothing else."

Raffi was silenced. He knew the importance of dreams, knew that Galen would clutch at anything that might help him.

"I can't ignore it, Raffi."

The Bee's Warning

"No," he mumbled unhappily.

They climbed up. The turf was springy, studded with yellow gorse-bushes. Warm, Raffi loosened the fastening of his dark green coat for the first time in days. The slope was steep; Galen stumbled once and picked himself up stubbornly. The dark grove hung above them, the rooks clamoring, disturbed. Anyone for miles would hear them. Catching his breath, Raffi stopped and looked back.

The downs stretched endlessly to the horizon. Great cloud banks hung, hazed with sunlight; white darkening to ominous gray, their slow rain-curtains dragged across the green land.

He turned and walked into the gloom of the trees. Yet as he passed the outer trunks he realized that this was not many trees, but one, immensely old, its trunk fibrous and dark, centuries old, maybe even older than the barrows.

Coming closer, they saw the central trunk was hollow; split wide enough for a small room. Trunk upon trunk had grown out of it, root upon root; the bark was ridged and scored, and Raffi guessed that six or seven men couldn't have joined hands around it. And yet it was alive. His feet sank in a thousand years of needles.

Around it, almost lost in gloom, stood three stones that might once have been some cairn or building. Pieces of rag hung from the branches. On one a piece of quartz swung and glinted in the sun.

"The Sekoi."

"Again."

Galen was bent under the thatch of branches. He put his hand on the central trunk. "How old this is. The secrets it knows. If I could . . ." He stopped himself. Then he sat down, closing his eyes.

"Galen," Raffi said anxiously. "How long are we going to stay here? We should get on!" There was no answer. Shaking his head, he sat down himself, against one of the outer trunks.

By late afternoon he was still there, watching the rain come. The gray curtain swept toward him over the downs, it swallowed the barrows and was on him, the first drops pattering in the thick green growth above, but none of it came through to him; the great yew was like a hut, its central trunk and pillars, its meshed roof. With the rain came the darkness, early. The rooks cawed and settled into a cowed silence. Nothing but the pattering of drops disturbed him. Glancing back stiffly he saw Galen still meditating, a shadow.

There was no way of lighting a fire; they were so high up it would be seen, and besides, he felt the tree wouldn't like it. Sitting there, against its back, he knew its hollows and veins and ridges; his fingers buried themselves in the woody debris, the crumbling rich stink of needles and grubs and tiny wriggling things that it nurtured. Nothing grew under here; it was too dark, but the tree's roots spread far out under the ground, he could feel them, widening to the nearest tombs, groping deep in the chalk, to the hidden waterlines, the fractures and fissures of rock, the strange magic that moved there. And the tombs clustered around it; he saw that now. The Sekoi had put their dead here, to watch with the tree.

And deep in his mind the tree said to him, *Raffi, get up and come in.*

He turned, thinking he'd misheard, but Galen was standing, looking at him, and though his face was in darkness there was something about him that gave Raffi a shiver of fear.

"What did you say?"

129

"I didn't say anything." The Relic Master stared at him in the gloom. His voice was dull with weariness.

"I thought . . . you said, 'Get up and come in.'"

Galen stiffened; then he got down in the soft mulch and grabbed Raffi's hood and hauled him closer. "It spoke to you!"

"I don't . . I'm not sure."

But Galen breathed out harshly. He turned to the inner trunk, the seamed split. "Sit there," he hissed, pushing Raffi down.

Don't fear me, the tree said, and its voice was old, textured like wind and rain on stone, the knock of a hammerbird in wood.

"It says not to be afraid."

"Afraid!" Galen had the threaded stones off his neck; he snapped the string, tipped them out, his long fingers arranging them hurriedly into patterns Raffi didn't know. Then he looked up, and his face was sharp and eager and desperate all at once. "Ask it to come out. To show itself. Tell it I can't see, or hear. Get it to come!"

Raffi barely knew how. Then training took over; he made a space in his mind, opened the third eye. *Please come out,* he asked, over and over. He knew it was close, and could hear him.

Galen crouched at his shoulder, his hand gripping tight. When Raffi looked now he saw rain, glinting on the trunk, dripping in places from above. The yew was huge; one edge of the split a bent contorted angle of wood, but as he looked closer he saw that he was mistaken, that it was a man, an old man in russet flaking, shapeless clothes, his eyes deep as knotholes, turning toward him.

Galen's fingers shook him.

"Has he come?"

Raffi nodded, silent.

The yew-man smiled at him and nodded too. *I've come, keeper.*

"He can't hear you," Raffi muttered, his throat dry.

How is that?

"There was an accident; he was hurt."

Glancing up, Raffi saw Galen's wild excitement. "Go on! Ask him! Can he help me!"

"There was an accident," Raffi said again, stumbling for words. "The keeper has lost . . . He can't enter the land now, or hear it when it speaks to him." He felt torn with awe at the yew-man's eyes, and embarrassment at Galen having to hear this.

The yew-man, too, seemed fascinated. He turned his brown old gaze on Galen, moved a fold of cloak to show two gnarled hands clasped on a root.

That must torment him. There is no loss as great as that.

"Yes . . ." Raffi wondered if Galen could hear. "Can you help? The yew is a tree of poison and healing. Do you have some way . . . ?"

No. The old man shook his head. *Only the Makers can give back what they have taken.*

"But the Makers are gone."

Tormented with impatience, Galen hissed, "What does he say about the Makers?"

But Raffi waved him back.

Yes, they are gone. The old man sighed. *I remember them, long since.*

"Remember them!"

I'm old, child, older than anything here. I guard the bones of the cat-kings, but before them all, I was. And when the Makers came and walked on the grass I saw

*them when they were young, Tamar and Therris and
Flain. Even Kest, whose sorrow burns us all. They could
have helped your master.*

"But . . ." Raffi grew dizzy; he shook his head, stunned.

"Hold on to it!" Galen's voice snapped. "Hold on!"

"The Makers are gone. We can't speak to them. The
only messenger was the Crow."

The Crow is still here, the yew-man said calmly.

"Here!"

*In this world. In this body. The Crow lives, for with-
out him the world would die.* The voice became slurred,
a harsh gabble of sound, then clear again. *Stone and tree
miss the keepers. Other men do not speak to us. We do
not know how to speak to them.*

The tree blurred before him.

"Hold on!" Galen muttered.

Sweating, dizzy, Raffi gripped his hands tight on the
old man's. "Where is the Crow?"

In Tasceron. In you. In your master, if he knew it.

"But where?"

The answer was harsh and garbled; the sound distorted
as if down tunnels and veins, deep in the earth. His hands

clasped a wooden knoll. He felt sick and retched, choking.

"Hold it!" Galen was yelling.

"I can't! He's gone! He's gone!"

Sweating, he was hauled up, dragged out from the tree on hands and knees. He collapsed in the grass, sick, shivering uncontrollably, his head throbbing with flashes of light and pain. After a while he realized Galen was holding him. Rain had soaked them both.

"Sorry."

"You did your best."

The keeper eased him against the tree, dragged the pack over, and pulled the blankets out. "Get these around you. It's aftershock. We should have a fire."

"Not safe."

"What did he say, Raffi?" Galen clutched him on both arms, as if he couldn't bear the suspense. "Can he cure me?"

Raffi shook his head. He looked away from the keeper's face.

"He remembered the Makers. He said . . . only they can give back what they've taken. He said the Crow is in Tasceron. And in us, if we knew it."

The Bee's Warning

"In us?" Then Galen stopped.

Another wave of nausea shuddered through Raffi. "What's wrong?" he croaked.

Galen had leaped up. He was looking down the hill, into the dark, and there was something in his look that made Raffi feel for his sense-lines.

They were all in shreds.

He staggered up and stood there, the blankets falling.

"Why don't you come up," Galen said grimly, "and see us from a little closer."

A dim shape was down there just beneath them, crouching on the dark turf.

"Come on!" Galen's voice was murderous.

The figure stood up, small and indistinct. Then the tiny moon, Pyra, came out. The light from it, ruby and warm, flickered over the girl.

The Watch, Unsleeping

11

*Once you believe, you are lost. Anything
you see or hear can be twisted against
you. The Order are masters of nothing
but falsehood.*

Rule of the Watch

SHE CAME A LITTLE CLOSER, then stopped.

"Is he all right?"

Galen glared at Raffi. "Is there anyone with her?"

Bewildered, Raffi groped for knowledge. "Only a horse, somewhere."

The girl stared at him in surprise. "You can hear it?"

He shrugged, uneasy.

She was small, wearing dark blue and gray trousers and jerkin, her hair a shiny nut-brown cut against her cheek. She seemed remarkably unconcerned.

As no one said anything, she went on, "My name is

141

Carys. Carys Arrin. I'm traveling west from here. Are you sure you're all right?"

Raffi was surprised. It was a long time since anyone had asked him that. "Fine," he said weakly.

"Why were you watching us?" Galen's voice was cold; Raffi felt the tension behind it. For a moment he felt sick again, and sat down abruptly.

"He's ill," the girl remarked accusingly.

Irritated, Galen glanced down. Then he hauled Raffi up and turned, his hawk-face dark against the rainy moon. "Come under the tree. We can talk."

Without waiting to see if she followed, he led Raffi in and sat him against the hollow trunk, tossing the blankets to him. Sensing the tree behind him made Raffi feel better, as if the strength of the wood and the spirit of it gave something back to him. His head cleared, and he looked up.

The girl stood hesitating under the thatch of branches. As she crouched he noticed the crossbow for the first time; it was wound back and loaded, he could see the bolt from here. She laid it on the dusty needles, but her hand stayed near it.

"I wasn't watching you. At least, not at first." She

glanced curiously around at the enormous bulk of the
yew. "I saw the trees and came up to see if I could shelter
here. The rain's getting heavy."

Galen said nothing. He was still standing, his head
bent under the low roof of twigs.

"Then I heard you talking." She shrugged. "I crept up.
I wanted to see who you were. You have to be careful,
traveling alone." Her fingers tapped the smooth shaft of
the bow.

"Indeed you do," Galen said. He sat down. "That goes
for us too."

She looked at him shrewdly. "I'm no threat to you. I
think I know what you are." As neither of them moved or
spoke, she shrugged again. "All right, I won't say it. But
no one else could have . . . It was very dark under here,
but I'm sure I heard him . . ." She glanced at Raffi and
shook her head, as if she couldn't get the words out.

"The tree spoke to him." Galen's voice was hard. "Is
that so difficult?"

"For some." She gave him a half smile.

After a moment he said, "Why travel alone?"

"I was with two friends of mine, but they turned back

at the last village. They'd heard stories about the Sekoi tombs on the downs, and that scared them off." She glared at her feet fiercely. "We had a terrible row and I stormed away. Told them I'd go on by myself. Then the rain came. They may be looking for me; but I doubt it. They had all the courage of jekkle-mice." She looked up suddenly. "You haven't got anything to eat, have you?"

Raffi's hopes plunged. Galen shook his head. "No. So where is it you're so eager to get to?"

For a moment she was silent, as if weighing him up. "I'm looking for my father." Her voice dropped. "The Watch took him."

Raffi peeled himself off the tree. "The Watch! Why?"

"Oh, you do speak, do you?" For a moment a laugh glinted in her face; then she turned it into the shadows. "I don't really know the answer to that. I wasn't there. When I came back to the village where we lived, he was gone. The Watchmen had come in the night—six of them, all armed, on black horses. They had broken the door down, dragged him out and taken him. It was so sudden . . ." Her voice was quiet; the rain outside hissed harder. Drops fell on Raffi's shoulder. "There was talk later that a man and a woman—travelers—had come to the house two days before. My father gave them a room, for one night. They paid him. There was nothing wrong with that. But if they were keepers . . ."

They were silent a moment. Raffi knew the Watch wouldn't have hesitated.

Carys looked up. "They came west, but I've lost the track. You would know, keeper. Where might they take him?"

Even Raffi wondered. But Galen said bleakly, "They want information. They'll get it out of him, then kill him. It's useless."

Stubbornly she shook her head. "I'm not giving up! Where?"

In the darkness of the tree the three of them had become dim shapes to one another. Galen's voice sounded strange. "I don't know. Maybe to Tasceron."

"Tasceron! Does it still exist?"

"It exists."

The rain was lessening. Slowly it pattered into silence, but the slow drops still fell here and there through the thick growth, branch to branch, steady and relentless, and the scents of the wet night rose in the after-storm hush.

Carys looked at them curiously. "Is that where you're going?"

Galen laughed harshly. "Us! It's the last place we'd want to go."

The girl was silent a moment. Then she said, "Look. Will you let me go on with you? I don't like being on my own. Not out here."

For a long moment the Relic Master watched the darkness outside. Then he said, "Until we reach a village, or a place you'll be safe. But we've no horses. We walk."

"So can I." Carys knelt up eagerly on the crushed needles. "Thank you. So now I won't need this." She lifted the bow.

"Maybe," Galen said stiffly. "Maybe we're not so safe as you think."

"I think you are." She stood up against the sky. "I'll bring my horse up." Then turning, she said, "You didn't tell me your names."

Galen looked into the dark. "Galen Harn," he said, his voice quiet. "And Raffael Morel."

When she was gone he looked across. "Well?"

Raffi pulled the blankets tight. He felt better now, but

tired. "She seems all right. And she's on her own. She won't be any threat."

"But is she telling the truth?"

"I don't know!" His throat was dry; he swallowed a few drops of rain from the ends of his fingers. "I don't know how to tell."

Galen was silent. "Once I knew when people were lying to me."

Raffi winced. The keeper turned on him suddenly as the horse harness clinked in the dark. "One thing. She's not to know about what happened to me. Understand? She's not to know!"

Sadly, Raffi nodded.

Journal of Carys Arrin
Agramonsnight
9.16.546

> The boy's asleep. Harn has drifted into some sort of trance; he sways and murmurs prayers in the dimness. I'm taking a chance but this book's small and easy to hide. It may be my last chance to write for a while.

First of all, the tree. I was lying out in the long grass—it was dark, but it seemed to me the boy was speaking to the tree and it was answering. I heard no words, but there was a sort of . . . tingle. I know this is heresy and I know it can't be real. But why make an illusion if they didn't know I was there? And the boy believed it.

I heard one thing that puzzled me. The boy distinctly said the Crow was in Tasceron. I remember the stories of the Crow from my training, but I'd always thought it was a figure of myth, a bird that talked. The bolt was on the crossbow; I had it aimed right at the middle of the keeper's back—but those words stopped me. After all, dead or alive are the orders. And they know something about this Crow. It may be the name of someone real, high in the Order, like an Archkeeper. A code name. It seemed worth a risk to find out.

So I let them see me. Harn is wary; he asked a lot of questions. I told them a story that would get them on my side, make us all enemies of the Watch. I was surprised how easy they were to deceive. The boy looked ill; they both seem half starved.

(Note for Jellie—the psychic defenses the

records mention can't exist. I'm certain they didn't know I was there.)

I'll try and stay with them as long as possible—to Tasceron, because I'm sure that's where they're going. I know the city is enormous, but if they find this Crow I'll be with them. To catch Harn and his boy would be good, but someone higher, a real chance to get into the secrets of the Order—that would make old Jeltok sit up. He always said I'd never make an agent.

I'm hungry, and the rain's started again. On foot we'll be slow. But they won't get rid of me now.

12

Tamar called the Sekoi to him and said, "We have brought life to the world, new trees, new animals. What gift have we for you, tall people?"

The Sekoi spoke among themselves. Then they said, "We ask no gifts of you. You are not our Makers. We were here before you. We will be here after you."

And Tamar was angry with the Sekoi, and turned them away.

Book of the Seven Moons

FOR TWO DAYS THEY TRAMPED the endless downs. They lived on water and whinberries and dried fish from the pack, and Raffi took it in turns with Carys to ride on the horse, which he enjoyed. Galen bluntly refused, and limped ahead.

Over the slow miles of chalk, Carys talked. She told him about her village, the school there, the ruined keeper's house beside it, and about her father, a small, shrewd man with red hair, though Raffi noticed if he asked too many questions she fell silent after a while. She must be worried sick, he thought guiltily.

The Sekoi tombs still bothered him. They were watchful, and eerie at night. Galen was silent most of the time. After the night at the tree he hurried them on, and Raffi knew that the promise of Tasceron tormented him, the lure of the Crow, of the cure he might find. He pushed them on all day till they were worn out, but even at night Raffi woke to see the keeper sitting up in the moonlight, turning the pages of the Book, while the were-birds moaned over his head.

"What's wrong with him?" Carys whispered once.

Alarmed, Raffi shook his head. "Nothing. And quiet, he'll hear."

"So? You seem scared of him."

He shrugged. "No. It's just . . . we've been through a lot."

"He doesn't treat you very well," she said archly.

"He doesn't treat himself very well."

"That's no excuse."

She had plenty to say and said what she thought. She made him laugh, and he hadn't done that for a long time. He realized how he had longed for company of his own age—at home there had been seven others. Though he'd missed them bitterly at first, he'd gotten used to Galen's morose silence. Or thought he had.

The Watch, Unsleeping

"How did you come to be a scholar?" she asked as they half slid down a slope of slippery grass, coaxing the horse. Galen was ahead, far below. Raffi pulled a face. "I lived on my mother's farm. There were eight of us."

"No father?"

"He'd died. Galen turned up one night, about four years ago." The sun broke through as he said it, and he had a dream-flash of his mother turning from the door, her eyes full of surprise, the man's gaunt shadow behind her. "He stayed three days. I remember how he watched all of us. He scared us a bit."

Carys grinned. "I'm not surprised."

"No . . . Then he picked me. He didn't say why. Just caught my arm one day and made me sit down and talk to him. Asked me about my dreams. Looked into my mind, my spirit-web."

Carys stumbled over a tussock. She brushed hair from her eyes. "He can do that?" she asked, her voice strained.

"Yes. At least . . . Well, sometimes." Raffi looked up at a wan yellow cloud blotting out the sun. "He asked me if I wanted to go with him."

155

She looked at him sidelong. "That's all? No payment?"

"Payment! Keepers have no money. My mother was honored, and I think a bit relieved. It's hard to feed eight. And as for me . . ." He shrugged. "I knew it would be dangerous, but that was exciting. And I wanted to learn. The Litany, the mind-webs, the opening and closing, all the rites and the Branches of power. I wanted that. I still do. I haven't learned half of it yet. They knew so much, Carys, these people! Before the Watch destroyed everything."

She was silent, nodding.

"The Watch are always after us. A while back I had a feeling they were on our trail. It's petered out now . . ."

"Raffi!"

Galen's yell was urgent. He was rigid, staring up at the sky.

Raffi raced down. "What is it?"

"That!"

Before them the sky was sour, a hissing yellow haze. It seemed to shift and swirl as if some enormous insect swarm blew toward them on the rising wind.

"Fireseed!" Carys breathed, beside him.

The Watch, Unsleeping

Galen nodded. "You've seen it before?"

"Heard of it."

So had Raffi, and the sight filled him with terror.

Once he had seen a man who'd only just survived a fireseed storm, his face burned and horribly scarred. Most weren't so lucky. Early in autumn, when the weather began to chill, the firepods exploded, the round spiked seed drifting, sometimes for days, in great poisonous clouds until they sank and grew into the dull reddish plants that were so common. There was nothing dangerous about the plants, but the seed would sear through the flesh it touched, the acid on the soft spines burning through leather and clothes. Kest's work. Like all the other evils.

Galen glanced around. There was no shelter. Only a few Sekoi barrows studded the turf.

The yellow cloud billowed.

"Run!" Galen turned. "Get on your horse, girl. Get out of here!"

He scrambled back up the slope; Raffi raced after him, grabbing handfuls of grass to haul himself up. Carys galloped ahead; she reached the ridge top and stared around hopelessly, the horse whickering with fear.

"Nothing! Not for miles!"

Galen pulled Raffi up. "The tomb. The nearest! Inside it!"

Despite the crackling cloud looming down on them, Carys paused. The horse pirouetted in terror. She had a sudden urge to gallop before the storm, away, abandoning them. But it was already too late. Scowling, she urged the beast toward the barrow.

Raffi was nearly there, Galen limping behind him. As she raced after them the storm swirled over her; glancing up she caught her breath at the yellow mass of seeds, billions of them, clotted like a rustling curtain. Something stung her face; she screamed, rubbing at it, jerking her head down on the horse's sweating neck.

The sky crackled around them. Galloping past Galen, she swung herself off. The barrow was a huge green swelling in the storm.

"How do we get in?" she screamed.

Seeds gusted around them, scattered on Galen's hood. He scrabbled at the edge of the mound, the row of sealing stones, tearing them away. She pulled too, and Raffi; something slid and rumbled, small stones falling in a dusty heap.

A black slit opened in the tomb like an eye. Raffi was gone, burrowing in, the pack dragged after him. "Now you!" Galen yelled.

Seeds fell on her shoulders; she squirmed and beat them off. "My horse!"

"We can't save it! Get inside!"

Pain stung her cheek. Desperately she dragged the maddened horse still; tore the small bag from the saddle. Then she was down, worming into the tiny black hole, stinging seeds kicked from her legs. Hands hauled her in. Galen's head and shoulders scrabbled through; then he was in, piling rocks in the entrance, and she glimpsed for a moment the air outside thick with poisonous flying drifts. The last stone blocked the gap.

"My poor horse," she whispered in the dark.

"Can't be helped." Galen's voice sounded hollow; it echoed around them. Raffi realized his skin was stinging; he rubbed his forehead and his fingers were burned, so that he hissed with the pain.

"Don't touch it," Galen's voice said. A sputter and crack came from the tinderbox; then a small flame lengthened to yellow. Galen's face and hands loomed out of the dark; he stuck the candle in a crevice and rummaged in the pack.

Raffi looked around, uneasy. He sensed that the chamber was small, too low to stand in. A roof of stone hung above; somewhere at the back of him was a low passageway, invisible. He let his mind grope into it. There were chambers down there, on each side. Traces of bones lingered in their dust. The last chamber, the one at the end, had something else in it.

He felt for it cautiously. Something very old.

Galen had the box of ointments out; he looked into Raffi's face. "Are we alone?"

"I don't think so."

Nodding, he thrust a small clay pot at Carys. "Then we'll have to hurry. Use this first."

She pulled the top off and dipped a finger in; it was cold and stiff, richly scented. Rubbing it on her hands and scorched face, she felt the seared skin cool; the relief was wonderful.

160

The Watch, Unsleeping

"What is it?"

"Never mind." Galen slapped it on his own hands, fingers over fingers. "Hurry up, Raffi. There are things to do."

When they had finished he cleared a space, lit seven candles and arranged them in a circle, working quickly. Carys felt uneasy. The new light showed a low passageway behind her, leading farther into the tomb. And though she told herself she was a fool, she felt with a prickling of her skin that there was something down there. "Raffi . . ." she began.

"We know." He looked up. "We know what to do."

He had poured water into a small silver dish, and now pulled out a red leather bag, full of objects. Despite her worry, excitement shivered through her. These were relics.

"Which one?" Raffi had his hand inside.

Galen thought quickly. "The bracelet."

He pulled it out. It was made of some smooth black leather, with a tiny fastening. Threaded on it was a strange flat slab of gold, studded with no stones, but with a gray window. Minute touch-buttons decorated the sides.

Carys edged nearer.

Raffi glanced at her. "Look at this." With his thumbnail he pressed one of the buttons hard. She stared, astounded. For a second, faint numbers had flickered in the window.

"What is it?"

"Who knows. It's almost dead now." Reverently he laid it down among the candles.

Galen had taken one string of black and green crystals from his neck; now he made a circle of it, around the relic. Then he and Raffi began to chant.

She recognized odd words, nothing more. This was the language of the Makers, long lost, except to the Order. It calmed her, made her feel strangely serene. It seemed important, here in the blackness of the tomb, though outside she would have laughed at it. But in this place something else lived, and she felt the strength of the chant, its protection, warming her, reassuring her. They'll have you believing all this, she told herself wanly. The crossbow lay under her hand, and she was glad it was loaded.

After the last response the silence was huge. Galen picked up the silver bowl and poured the water gently into the ground. "We bring you a gift, guardian," he said. "We're not here to disturb you. We don't break the sacred lines."

Raffi could feel them, the earth-lines. They reached out, one north, two to the west, another, very old and faint, southwest. Invisible, underground. As Galen dug a deep slot in the ground and buried the relic in it, Raffi felt a pulse along the lines, a faint crackle of power.

The Sekoi had taken the gift.

That seemed to be all. Carys sat back against the wall, almost impressed. The ritual had drawn it away, that air of threat in the dark chamber behind her. Or had she imagined the whole thing? Shaking her head, she glanced down at the bag with the journal in it. That and the cross-bow were all she had left. She was really undercover now.

They stayed where they were, not exploring. They drank water, chewed the last of the fish, maybe even slept a little. Raffi wasn't sure. The darkness confused them; they seemed deep, deep underground. Time seemed still. There was no way of knowing if the storm had ended. Maybe it had finished hours ago. And yet none of them moved.

Lying there, Raffi began to imagine he saw scrawls and carvings on the stones overhead, spirals that swirled if he stared at them, so that he looked away, uneasy, and when he looked back they had shifted.

Galen sat huddled, resting forehead on arms. Carys was silent, as if the barrow swallowed her words before she spoke them. Raffi gathered his strength. With a great effort he managed to say, "It may be safe now."

Instantly they all felt hours had been lost. Galen looked up, his face haggard in the candlelight. "What are we doing! Look outside!"

Raffi dragged the stones free. A small draft blew into the chamber; the light outside seemed dim. Late afternoon, Carys thought, rubbing her face. Raffi's head and shoulders blocked the hole. Then he squirmed back inside. "It's stopped. But the seeds are lying all over the ground."

They crawled out one by one and stood stiffly. The tomb rose in a sea of yellow; the scattered seed lay in a clogged mat all around them, as far as they could see on the downland. Here and there swathes of grass were clear, or the fall was light, but in places the poisonous carpet looked almost solid.

The Watch, Unsleeping

"Can we get through that?" Carys muttered.

"We have to." Galen pulled the pack on and gripped his stick. "Follow me close."

Hurriedly blocking the barrow-hole behind them, Raffi took a last glimpse inside. For a moment he felt the sense of something else there, staring at him out of the dark. He jammed a stone in the gap and jumped back.

Galen was stepping carefully through the fallen seeds. He headed west, and went quickly, because there was no knowing how many miles the seedfall stretched, and to be caught in the middle of it on only a two-moon night might be disastrous. But avoiding the densest clots meant they had to circle far out of their way, placing their feet carefully among the seared grasses. Close up, Raffi saw the seeds were fist-sized balls of spikes that rolled in the breeze; sometimes a few gusted up in the air, and the travelers had to stop and watch them anxiously. It was slow, treacherous work, and they knew the corrosive acids were eating into the leather of their boots at every step.

They had walked for two hours and were weary of it when they came to the top of a rise and saw the sunset blazing the sky before them. Something else made Raffi jerk up his head like a fox.

"Galen!" he said.

It was too late. Below, looking up at them in surprise, were three men, two on horseback and one walking.

They were armed, and their horses were painted in dark reds and black. They were the Watch.

13

Even across the dark, even across the loss, even across the emptiness, soul will speak to soul.

Poems of Anjar Kar

CARYS STOOD STILL. She decided to do nothing and say nothing. For a start, she wanted to know how Galen dealt with this, whether the keepers really did have the mind-weapons legends spoke of. And if they escaped, she needed to stay with them.

One of the Watchmen called them down. She was surprised when Galen laughed sourly. Raffi looked terrified.

The Watchman yelled again.

Galen raised a hand and nodded. "There's a village beyond the trees," he muttered, glancing at the smoke. "If they ask, we come from there."

Making his way down between the scattered seeds, he

169

looked sidelong at Carys. "If we're found out, tell the truth. You fell in with us two days ago. You don't know who we are."

She grinned at him, tucking her hair behind her ear. "Oh don't worry about me. I'm good at lying."

"I'm sure you are," he said coolly.

The seed was thin here; they were at the edge of it. The Watchpatrol waited for them. They were well armed, Raffi noticed, wearing a patchwork of body armor. One had a helmet, badly dented. His heart was hammering in his chest; desperately he wished he knew what Galen was up to. He'd learned to fear that cold laugh.

Close up, they saw the men had hardly outridden the storm. They were all burned, and in pain; one had his arm bound up and gripped it tight. And they must have lost a horse.

"Good evening," Galen called out cheerily. Carys glanced at him in astonishment.

The Watchsergeant, the one on foot, looked them over.

"Where have you come from?" he growled. "Out of the downs after a fire-fall?"

Galen leaned on his staff. "There are places to shelter

if you know them. You obviously weren't so lucky."

"We'd have been dead if it hadn't stopped." The man was big, stolid, but shrewder than the other two, who seemed in too much pain to be curious. Carys knew his sort. He'd be suspicious.

"Who are you?" he asked.

"My name is Harn," Galen said recklessly. "These are my children, Raffael and Carys." He put his arm around her and squeezed. She smiled up happily at the Watchman and thought that Galen could tell lies as well as she could. He was far more cunning than she'd thought. She'd have to be more careful.

"You come from the village there?"

"We do," Galen said confidently.

"Then take us there. My men are hurt."

They should have been ready for it. It was a staggering blow, but Galen didn't flinch. He nodded, falling into step beside the Watchsergeant, talking about the seeds as if he hadn't a care in the world. Grudgingly the Watchman listened as he walked. The two on horses trailed behind. Neither would be any problem, Raffi thought; he knew enough to terrify horses. But the third!

They should jump him now. What was Galen doing!

Carys was beside him, her bow slung on her back. "He's mad. What's his plan?"

"I don't know." Raffi stared at his master's back. "He gets like this sometimes. Does reckless things. You can't talk to him. Sometimes I think he's trying to get himself killed."

She stared at him. "Are you serious?"

"He looks for trouble. At least since the accident—" He stopped.

"What accident?"

He shrugged. "A relic exploded. He was hurt."

"His leg, you mean?"

Raffi nodded. He didn't seem to want to say any more.

She looked away, at the seeds on the stubble-field. "Not much of a reason for getting killed."

He didn't answer. She knew there was something important here; something he wasn't telling her, but before she could try again they were in the muddy lane between the first houses. A group of villagers were brushing fire-seed into a heap. When they saw the travelers, they stood stock-still.

The Watch, Unsleeping

"Too late anyway," Carys muttered. She unslung her bow, annoyed, glancing back at the stumbling horses. Galen Harn was hers. No one else was bringing him in, certainly no potbellied sergeant. "Get ready."

Raffi shook his head. "You're not in this."

"I am now."

The Watchsergeant strode up to the villagers; most of them fell back, leaving a thin gray-haired man in a patched brown coat as the spokesman. He nodded grimly. "So you're back."

"We said we would be," the sergeant snarled.

"We were afraid the seeds might have killed you." The man's voice was acid.

The sergeant gave him a small sour smile. "Well, they haven't."

"Haven't you had enough from us!" a woman screamed from the crowd. "Where is my son? Where is he?"

"You know where they are." The sergeant drew his sword easily, sensing the rising tension. "In good hands. The Watch will feed them, clothe them, and they'll be taught. More than you could have given them. You should bless the Watch."

"And now you've come for more." The gray-haired man gripped his hands around the rake handle.

"No. You've given your quota. We're only here because the storm caught us out." He half turned. "We met your friends here on the down. They've been lucky as well."

The villagers stared.

Carys gripped her bow.

Galen glanced briefly at Raffi. Carys was close; she heard Raffi barely whisper the word. "Arno."

The keeper strode forward, slapping an arm around the villager's shoulder. "Arno! Good to see you. How have things been?"

Amazed, Carys watched. For a moment Arno was silent, stiff with surprise. He won't do it, she thought. Her fingers slid the bolt in. Behind her, Raffi waited, hands gripped tight.

Then Arno spoke. "They've been fine," he said. His voice was dry; his face held no flicker of astonishment. "We've been expecting you, brother. Here's your wife."

Galen took a step back. He looked wary at once; his face darkened. A woman ran out of the crowd, tall and fair-haired; she flung her arms around him and kissed him. "You're back! And early too!" She came to Raffi and Carys and grabbed their hands. "You both look half starved. I've got some fine chickens roasting for you, just as you like them . . ." Talking and laughing and not letting them answer, she led them briskly between the houses, away from the crowd. Glancing back, Raffi saw the Watchmen dismounting, the sergeant giving orders.

Around the corner Galen stopped the woman. "What's going on!"

She shook her head impatiently. "I should ask you that! How could you just walk in here with them! And why haven't you been answering me? For two days I've been trying to make you hear."

He stared at her, his dark eyes narrowing with delight. "You're a keeper!"

"Of course I am. Now in here. Quickly!"

She pushed them through a low doorway into the house. Straightening, Raffi saw a long room with another beyond it, a bright fire crackling, a complicated arrangement of spits with three chickens being turned by a very old woman who grinned at him, showing only one tooth.

"Is this them?" she asked.

"Yes." The tall woman looked back through the slit of the door. "No one seems to be following. The Watch are back."

The old woman spat. "God curse them."

"Arno will keep them busy. Go and keep an eye on them."

The old hag winked, and pulled a shawl around her head. She slid silently through the door.

"Can we trust her?" Galen asked.

"Of course I can, she's my mother. Now, leave your pack. Sit down. The first thing is to get you something to eat."

Raffi watched her slice the meat. Suddenly he knew he was starving. The hiss of the grease dropping in the flames, the smell of it, tormented him. As she worked, the woman said quickly, "My name is Lerin. I was a scholar of the Order. My master was taken and killed."

"His name?"

"Marcus Torna.

Galen nodded somberly. "I knew of him."

"I escaped. I don't think the Watch knew he had any pupils with him. I had nowhere to go, so I came home.

The Watch, Unsleeping

Here. Ten years ago now. The people here are my family. They despise the Watch, more so now than ever. Those men were here three months ago. They took ten children, all under five, for their filthy Watchhouses. God knows what will happen to them."

She thrust a plate of meat at Raffi. "Think of it! Our own children, drilled and trained and warped into our enemies. The brightest, the cleverest!" She paused, staring at Galen. "What future do those children have? Their mothers are distracted with grief."

He shook his head heavily. Carys sat staring at the fire so hard that Raffi nudged her. When she looked at him, just for a moment, something flickered in his mind, a drift of pain. As he reached for it, it was gone.

She glared at him. "Leave me alone, Raffi."

The woman looked at her suddenly. "Who are you? I didn't know about you."

"We met her," Galen muttered. "On the downs." He sat down on a bench, as if he was suddenly weary.

Lerin glanced at him. Then she stood upright, the knife still in her hand. "Why didn't you answer me, keeper? I have sense-lines—good ones—flung right out into the downs. Two days ago you walked through the first. I searched for your mind. I was nearly a Relic Master— only a few more months with Marcus and I would have made the Deep Journey. I know what I'm doing. Why didn't you answer me?"

Galen lifted his head. He faced her across the room, the fiery shafts of the last sunlight slanting between them. "I think we should talk about this later. Alone. Many things have happened. But I am who you think I am. Galen Harn. Relic Master."

For a moment they looked at each other, and the sun faded. Then the woman's face changed; Carys thought she seemed astounded, and then horrified. "Can it be . . . ?"

"Later!" Galen looked away into the dark. "I'll explain later."

Journal of Carys Arrin
Karnosnight
11.16.546

I thought Raffi would burst, he ate so much.
Mind you, so did I. Now he's asleep and so is Galen.
After the meal everyone was too tired to talk.

The Watch, Unsleeping

Tomorrow, the woman said. The Watchpatrol may have moved on then. She's out, but the old woman is somewhere about.

Something's wrong. He has to ask Raffi for information. The villager's name. Why didn't he know it? Why not answer the woman's mind-call?

Maybe he's a fraud. Maybe the powers of the Order are nothing—and yet she would know that.

Maybe he suspects me.

He's a harsh, strange man, and sees far. And yet he went deliberately into danger. I don't understand what's happening here. But I'll find out.

All right. The real reason I'm writing is that I can't sleep. Why did she have to say that, about those children? Did I come from a village like this? Was my mother distracted with grief? I always thought, before, that Watchchildren were orphans . . . I never thought . . .

This is stupid. I'm going to sleep.

Note: Information about Lerin would be useful to the Watch. I don't think I'll send it.

14

What does the keeper know?
The secrets of the world.
To whom does the keeper speak?
God and the Makers.
What does the keeper fear?
Nothing but despair.

Litany of the Makers

"TASCERON!"

Lerin stared at them in amazement. "Galen, you can't go there! It's madness!"

He brooded across the firelit room. Outside, the cold rain fell heavily, splatting the pocked track into mud. Washed, full of food, and after the best night's sleep he'd had for months, Raffi watched the keeper anxiously. Galen was gaunter these days, his hair long and ragged, his hawk-nose jutting, eyes dark with obsession. Now he turned the cup of ale on the table, tracing the pattern on the leather.

"Maybe it is. But there are reasons for it. The first is the girl's father."

Carys blinked. For a moment she had forgotten her own story.

Lerin looked at her and shook her head. "I'm sorry, but that's . . . well, you have to face facts. He may well be dead already."

"I don't care," Carys said. "I'm going to find out!" She glanced at Galen. "Tell her your other reasons."

He drank, and set the cup down. Then he said, "I'm looking for a Sekoi. Brindled fur, with a zigzag under the eye. A man called Alberic wants him."

"Why?"

"Alberic has a relic of ours. A crystal box that emits light. That can kill."

Carys tried not to stare. She leaned back in the soft comfort of the chair, hoping he'd say more about it, but Lerin didn't seem very surprised. "And he says he'll give it back in return for the Sekoi?"

Galen shrugged. "So he says. I doubt it."

"Then why bother looking for the creature at all!" She came and sat on the bench opposite him, her long red skirt trailing in the soot. "Keeper, you can trust me. Tell me your real reason. No one goes to the Wounded City for nothing."

For a long moment he looked at her.

"I think you should," Raffi blurted out.

"No one asked you, boy."

"They never do. But I'm the one who'll have to go with you!"

Galen was silent. Then he looked over. "Carys. This is not for you to hear. Wait outside."

She glared. "I'm going to Tasceron too!"

"For your own reasons. This doesn't concern you."

She shrugged, and looked at Lerin. "It's a bit wet to wait outside."

The tall woman nodded. "Go in the other room. My mother is there."

Reluctantly Carys got up. As she crossed the room and turned to close the door, Raffi had a glimpse of her face. To his astonishment, just for a moment, he saw that she was furious.

When the door closed, Lerin leaned forward. "Now," she said. "What happened to you?"

Galen was silent; when he spoke his voice was strained. "Ten months ago the boy and I were called to a settlement in the forest, well east of here. They had come across a relic, a huge, strange thing, and had kept it hidden from the Watch. When I saw it, I was astonished. It was tall, tubular, and had once stood upright in the ground. Now it lay fallen. A great rusted mass.

"I knew at once that power was still in it and that it was dangerous. After the Makers had gone, many of their devices ran out of control. This one was evil. I told the boy to move the people away. I opened my mind to it, saw it, all the colors and lights about it, all the threads of power. Then I came closer. Carefully, I touched it."

He sat back and laughed bleakly. "That's all I remember."

She glanced at Raffi, wide-eyed.

"It exploded," he said quietly. "The noise! It was incredible. The forest burned; the villagers fled, most of them. I ran back, though my nose and ears were bleeding. Galen was lying there. For a moment I thought he was dead . . ."

"I was dead." Galen's voice was harsh. "I still am. It's

gone, keeper, all of it. I have only two eyes like other men, and see nothing more than they do. When the wind blows in the trees I hear only the wind. Nothing more. The traces of the Makers are lost. My mind is a great silence."

"Nothing?"

"No bird-speech, no earth-lines, none of the world's million voices. No mind-speech. No dreams."

She watched him closely, full of horror; Raffi could feel it seeping from her like a musky scent. "How do you survive?" she whispered.

"Prayer," he said bleakly. "And whatever the boy can do."

She was silent, plaiting the folds of her red skirt with her fingers. "And you think in Tasceron there might be someone left to help you?"

"More than that." He glanced at the door. "Where are the Watch?"

"Saddling up. They don't suspect anything. They don't know everyone here, and these two are too old for their Watchhouses." She pulled a face. "I hope they'll have forgotten you by next time."

Galen nodded. He shuffled a little closer, the flames edging his face with shadow. "Twice," he said quietly, "we've had word of something very strange. Both messages were the same—that the Crow is alive, and in the city."

"The Crow! Impossible!"

His face darkened with anger. "Don't call me a liar! Marcus Torna couldn't have taught you that."

"I'm sorry." Lerin shook her head ruefully. "I'm sorry, keeper, I was wrong. Nothing is impossible to God. But the Crow! I thought . . . nothing of the Makers is left whole. Why should he be left?"

"Why not?" Galen got up abruptly, as if he couldn't sit still any longer. He prowled to the window and stared out at the rain. "Why not? The Makers have gone, but they knew the future. They may have foreseen the destruction of the Order. They may have left us their messenger, buried deep under the ruins, for us to find him when we need him most!" He turned urgently. "It's an omen, Lerin, I know it is! The Crow can cure me, maybe, but more than that, he can cure the world. He can rid us of the Watch!"

A tiny sound at the door made Raffi stiffen. But Galen hadn't heard it and Lerin was thinking deeply and gave no sign. Raffi could feel Carys close. Perhaps she was listening. But he wasn't bothered about that, the relief was so great. Now someone else knew. And surely Lerin would try to talk him out of it. She had to.

After a while she looked up.

"You think I'm on a fool's errand," Galen said drily.

She shrugged. "Perhaps I do. On the other hand I can see why you have to go. If it could be true . . ."

"It is! I'm sure of it."

She frowned. "But keeper, think of the immensity of Tasceron! There are a million streets, whole warrens of ruined districts. Flames burst from the ground; the air is always black. It would take a lifetime to search, even to stay alive."

"We'll be told where to look." Galen was obstinate. "There will be messages. We just need faith."

She nodded, rather sadly. Perhaps she realized, as Raffi did, finally and hopelessly, that Galen had made up his mind and nothing would change it. Perhaps she knew he could only stay sane if he had some hope.

She stood up, the green and blue awen-beads slipping against her neck. "You'll need a ship. We trade with a

RELIC MASTER: THE DARK CITY

village on the coast—a day's walk from here. There's a harbor there; ships cross the Narrow Sea. We'll get you on one."

"The Watch."

"Don't worry. As I said, the people here are my family."

"I'm grateful," Galen said with a grim joy.

"One thing." The woman faced him. "I have a feeling of foreboding on me, keeper. Dark dreams came to me all night, and I fear you may be walking to your death. So I give you this warning from the Makers. Your life is sacred. The knowledge you have is sacred. You have no right to throw it away in defiant risks. Above all, you have no right to risk the boy's life. There have been enough martyrs. Hear this, Galen Harn."

Her voice had changed and darkened. Raffi shivered. All at once she seemed full of some authority that made her face grave and beautiful, and yet was gone in an instant, as if someone else had been there.

"I hear." Galen bowed his head, shaken and uneasy. "I hear you, lords."

190

The Watch, Unsleeping

THEY STAYED IN the village for two days, eating well and sleeping late. The Watch had gone, taking three goats, some chickens, and the curses of the villagers. Now they nodded to the travelers with quiet respect. Raffi was used to this but it amused Carys.

"They really think you're special."

He looked at her, surprised. "So they should. Most people still have respect for the Order."

Cursing herself, she nodded. "I know that."

They walked on among the houses, the hens squawking away. She thought back to the mumbles of conversation she had heard through the door, once the wretched old woman had finally dozed off. The Crow again. But more, some things she'd missed.

"Raffi," she said suddenly. "How did you know Arno's name?"

He was watching three children play in a puddle. Their mother came out and smacked them. "Names are easy," he said. "They lie on the surface, like a tiger-flower. Bright, with deep roots."

"So why did Galen have to ask you?"

He glanced at her angrily. "You don't know much

about keepers, Carys. He's always testing me. I'm his pupil." He looked away. "Let's climb the hill. I'll race you to the top." And he ran, clambering over the rocks, jamming his feet in the rabbit holes, not waiting to see if she followed, because he hated lying to her, and was ashamed of it.

The weather was sunny, with sudden autumnal crashes of rain. Galen spent much time meditating, and once Lerin took him and Raffi to her relic hoard, in a secret cave in the chalk-country.

In the evenings they talked around the fire, and the keepers took turns to tell stories of the Makers: the adventures of Flain in the Land of the Dead; Kest's great fight with the Dragon of Maar, whose tail tore half the stars from the sky.

Half asleep, warm against the back of a cushioned chair, Raffi dreamed, seeing the scenes of the stories vaguely in the flames and flickering light—the caves and hollows of the underworld, the Sekoi ghosts, the passageways and treasure rooms. Once he watched Carys listening, and was caught by something in her face, some far-off look, till she saw him and frowned.

The Watch, Unsleeping

Part of him wanted to stay in the village forever, but on the third day Lerin told them everything was ready.

"You go tomorrow, with the trade goods. Fleeces, barley, honey, apples. Arno will go with you. The ship is called the *Sigourna*, and she'll be waiting at Troen—that's the harbor. She's sailing to the Morna River—the nearest place to Tasceron we can get you."

Galen nodded. "Good, Lerin! Excellent."

She glanced at Raffi, who just shrugged. He knew that what he thought didn't matter.

15

*One day Flain walked in the Forest of
Karsh and he was thirsty. Coming to
a stream, he drank, and such was his
strength that the ground sank lower.
He went on his way. The sea rose and
drowned the forest.*

*Though the Sekoi have another story
about this.*

Book of the Seven Moons

THE ALLEYWAY WAS DARK and there was something else in it. Jammed against the damp wall, Raffi heard it swoop out of the darkness. He turned and ran, through cobwebs that webbed his face and hands as he brushed them away.

The floor rose; he tripped, fell flat. The thing was on him, its sharp claws raking his back, its stinking breath on his neck. He yelled and squirmed and was up again, running blindly into the blackness till the wall smacked against him and he crumpled, breathless, fighting, struggling, kicking off blankets, his coat, the strong fingers that grabbed at him again and again.

"Raffi! Keep still! It's me. For Flain's sake, get yourself under control!"

The roar was Galen's and it woke him instantly, just before Carys came hurtling around the door into the cabin, her shirt hanging out. "What's the matter? Is he seasick?"

"No." Galen let him go and sat back. "I don't think so."

"Of course I'm not! It was a dream." Raffi rubbed sweat from his face. "A nightmare."

Under them the ship dipped and sank. His stomach lurched, and a tray of cups and plates slid slowly down the tilted table.

"All dreams count," Galen said, grabbing the edge of the chair. "Tell it to me."

Raffi shrugged. "I was in some sort of street . . ." He explained briefly, bringing the dream accurately out of memory as Galen had taught him. When he'd finished, Carys grinned. "It was that cheese you ate."

Galen frowned at her. "It may be important. Remember it."

The ship rose suddenly; the oil lamp swung, sending

wild shadows over the low ceiling. Carys sat down and laced her boots.

"Still lost."

They had been at sea for two days, and the weather had gotten steadily worse. Halfway over, the fog had come down. Now the tiny cabin was dim with it; it drifted down the steps, making the lamp a cloud of haze; the rough blankets smelled of its damp.

It was late morning, but morning and night all seemed the same.

"Have they asked again?" Raffi asked quietly.

"They will," Galen muttered.

Almost as an answer there was a bang on the open door; Arno came in, bending his head. He looked harassed and soaked. "I'm sorry, Galen."

He stood aside; behind him the skipper blocked the door, a small, black-bearded man, his cap in his hand. He twisted it nervously. "Keeper, the men are scared. The fog's too thick, we don't know how near the shore we are. The Watch patrol this strait, and if they come on board . . ."

"I know," Galen said heavily. "We're bringing you into danger."

"It's just that some of the older men . . . they say the Order had weather-warding skills. I don't know. But if there's anything you can do . . ."

Galen was silent a moment. Carys watched him curiously. Then he said, "I'll come on deck. First I have to prepare."

The two men backed out respectfully and Carys went with them, climbing the steps to the deck and pulling her blue coat around her. The fog was iron-gray and hung close; it tasted metallic and salty. She could barely see the ship's rail till she bumped into it; above her the masts dissolved into dimness. Even the sea, invisible below, was silent, rising and falling as smooth as oil, the only sounds a tarred rope dragging, canvas creaking, the murmur of voices in the gloom.

Then Galen and Raffi came up. The keeper had a small object in his hand; it looked like quartz crystal. Raffi looked nervous, she noticed. Galen shoved a coil of rope aside and laid the crystal on the soaked planks of the deck; with some chalk he drew strange signs around it, some of which she recognized from her training. A bird, the seven sigils of the moons, a slashed circle, a bee.

The Watch, Unsleeping

Behind her the sailors gathered, like wraiths in the fog.

Galen straightened. Then he beckoned, and Raffi came forward. He looked pale in the dimness.

"Aren't you going to do this?" the captain asked anxiously.

Galen stared at him in surprise. "Weather-warding is a task for scholars," he said curtly. "Not masters."

He nodded to Raffi, who took a deep breath, closed his eyes, and spread out his hands. Below him the crystal lay wrapped in fog.

Carys watched closely. For a while nothing happened and she told herself it wouldn't. The whole thing was nonsense. Someone whispered behind her, and Galen growled "Be quiet" without looking over. She saw he was staring at Raffi intently, as if willing him on. The ship sailed silently into darkness. And then a tiny thrill of fear tingled in Carys's spine; she clenched her fingers, breathing in sharply.

Around the crystal, the fog had gone.

A tiny circle of empty air hung there, the white stone glinting, the knots on the shaven planks clear and sharp. Raffi opened his eyes and grinned. He looked dazed and delighted. The circle grew; the fog rolled back, was pushed apart, and men murmured and whistled in subdued awe. Now they could all see one another, then the wide deck, now the opposite rail with a gull that flew off with a shriek of alarm, and still the circle of power swelled. Carys stood rigid, watching. There was the mast, the rigging, the ship's cat in the high spars; they were all appearing in this great bubble of clearness. Turning to the rail, she looked down and could see the sea, the green splash of it, out to the receding wall of the mist. She shook her head, bewildered. "Oh, Jeltok. What would you say about this?"

"Who?" Raffi stood behind her, smiling.

"No one. You look pleased."

He laughed. "I feel it! I've never done it so well!"

"Brilliant!" The skipper had crammed his cap on and seized Galen's hand. "Brilliant!"

Galen snatched his hand away. "Not me. The boy."

"Of course!" Clapping Raffi carelessly on the back, the man stared at the sea. "How big will it grow?"

"About half a league around the ship will be clear. Beyond that the fog remains." Galen crossed to Raffi and looked down at him. Stiffly he said, "Well done."

The Watch, Unsleeping

Raffi was astonished. "The way the power moves through your hands . . ." he murmured.

Galen almost flinched. Then he said, "I know."

"I didn't mean . . . I'm sorry . . ."

"Quiet!" The keeper turned on him fiercely. "That's enough!"

Carys watched them. Then she turned and looked out at the circle of fog, a clear rim. And she saw, growing out of the sea, a forest of huge blackened trees, straight and bare, their branches high above, arching like tunnels over the green swell.

"What's that!"

Galen glared at it savagely and didn't answer. At her back, Arno murmured, "The drowned forest. The Forest of Karsh."

She had heard of it. The great black trees rose like pillars, their roots deep underwater, and as they sailed close to one she saw the hardness of the wood, fossilized and ridged, like rock.

"Are they alive?" she whispered.

"They must be. I can feel them," Raffi said. Then he winced, as if he'd been stung.

"What's the matter?"

"Sense-lines. Something's coming!" He spun around to Galen. "Behind us. A ship. Very close!"

"Watchpatrol!" The skipper turned and leaped up the steps to the upper deck, yelling frantic orders. A new sail plumped out. The ship shuddered and slewed.

"You'll never outrun them," Carys muttered. She stared back. "I can't see anything."

"They're there." Galen slammed the rail in fury; then he turned and yelled, "Into the trees! Take us into the trees!"

"Keeper, I can't!" The skipper stared down at him, aghast. "No one sails in there! There are no soundings— no one has ever mapped all the shoals and currents, the channels . . . And God knows what lives in there!"

With a mutter of fury, Galen raced up the steps and caught him by the coat. "And what happens when the Watch sail out of the fog? Do you think they won't know a weather-warding when they see it? Get in there before they see the name of your ship! Or do you want to be rammed out of the water!"

The man stared at him, white-faced. Then he twisted.

The Watch, Unsleeping

"Hard aport! Get that topmast gallant down! Do it!"

Slowly, unwillingly, the ship turned; sliding toward the dark gap between the two nearest trees.

"Wouldn't it be easier to bring the fog back?" Carys said uneasily.

Raffi shook his head. "Can't. Not now. The spell will last for hours."

"Then they'll always be able to tell where we are."

"If they come in after us."

"Oh, they'll come in," she muttered.

The gap widened. As they entered it, a green dimness fell over their faces; high above them the stark branches stirred and they saw that dim leaves hung in strange clusters. In here it was dark, the only sounds the grunts of men furling the heavy sail and, looking behind them, Raffi saw the open sea beyond the entrance to their tunnel, the ship's wake sending ripples and swell slapping and clooping against the black rigid columns of the trees.

And then, just where the mist ended out there, he glimpsed the prow of a ship breaking out into the sunshine, the great silver eye painted on its side staring at him over the green water, and he shuddered, as if something had seen right to the heart of him.

Then they turned among the trees, and the daylight was blocked.

"Did they see us?"

"Who knows," Galen growled. "If they did, they'll come."

It was eerily silent, but for the wave-slap, the echoes. On each side of them the trees rose like black pillars in some gloomy, flooded hall; a forest waist-deep in dark water, stretching into dimness, stinking of decay, the crisp leaves rustling overhead. How strong they must be, Raffi thought, still growing as they had a thousand years ago, as if they'd never noticed the sea that drowned them.

The ship was deep inside now. The light was a green gloom; strange birds whistled. The branches over his head swished, as if some invisible creature leaped and followed. The skipper hung over the water, watching, afraid of a crash. The ship moved on mysterious currents, without any wind they could feel. Raffi saw how the crew clustered together, staring in fear into the depths of the still, drowned trees. Of the Watchship they could see nothing, and no daylight either. The deeper in they went, the darker the trees became.

Galen stirred. "How near are we to the coast?"

The skipper shook his head despairingly. "Who knows! Almost aground, maybe. The forest comes ashore south of Tasceron, according to the charts, but whether we can get the ship that close . . ."

"You'll have to," Galen said. He turned to Raffi. "Well?"

"They're still coming. Maybe getting closer."

"Right. Get below and get our things. You too, Carys, if you're coming."

"Of course I am!"

Below, in the cabin, jamming her journal deep into her bag she said, "What's he going to do?"

"I daren't think." Raffi checked the relic bag gloomily.

Abruptly, the ship shuddered. The sudden jarring shock sent them both crashing; cups and plates and a lamp slid and smashed on top of them.

Carys picked herself up painfully. "She's gone aground! Come on!"

On the deck, uproar had broken out. Men were running, yelling orders, the ship tilted at a bizarre angle, one side high out of the water. Scrambling up to the rail, Raffi clung there and saw that a huge splintered tree trunk was jammed under them; beyond it a tangle of roots, immense, a gloom of mudbanks.

"Here will do," Galen said. He slung the pack on his shoulder and jammed his staff across it; then he climbed up onto the rail.

"We can't just leave them!" Raffi yelled. "Not like this!"

Galen glared at him coldly. "They don't need us. We're just a danger for them. Do you want the Watch to find us on board?"

Poles were out; the sailors had them over the side and were heaving on them, the small ship shuddering and grinding.

"Now!" Galen said. "While we can." He swung his legs over, steadied himself and jumped onto the black, slippery mass of wood, almost fell, then pulled himself quickly upright. Carys followed carefully, then Raffi, letting himself down by his arms. Just as he let go, the ship juddered free. Arno's white face came to the rail. "Galen, there's no need . . ."

"This is as far as we go." Galen looked into the forest quickly. "Get away from here. Tell Lerin I'll remember what she said."

Arno nodded. "Good luck. Keep safe." He leaned closer. "Give us your blessing, keeper."

Galen spoke the words softly, his hand stretched out. For a moment they watched the ship drift away between the black trees. When he turned, the keeper's voice was quiet. "The bravery of the faithful. Remember it, Raffi."

The three of them had to crawl and slide along the huge trunk, the rounded surface slippery but wide as a track. Halfway to the jutting roots, Carys flattened herself. "Get down!"

Alarmed, Raffi jerked, grabbed, and slid hopelessly off into the water, trying not to splash. Chin-deep he hung on, scrabbling for a hold, finding to his astonishment that his feet touched bottom, sinking into deep mud. Small gnats whined about him; the water stank and he closed his lips tight not to swallow any.

The Watchboat came through the drowned forest in silence, a sleek, black-painted ship, sharp-prowed, her silver eye glinting in the green light. She moved quickly, drawn by the current; on board Raffi could see men in the rigging and on the decks, leaning out, looking anxiously down.

Still as leaf-shadow, they watched the enemy pass, the wake sending tiny waves to lap against Raffi's lips. He turned away.

Finally, when she was gone, Galen sat up, his stare full of hate. "I hope they outrun her." He leaned over and grabbed Raffi's arm; tugging his feet free, Raffi gasped, "I can't get up. Too slippery. I'll wade."

Splashing as little as possible, he struggled along the side of the trunk; to his relief the water quickly became shallower until it was down to his waist. He shivered, rubbing off green slime, water running from his clothes.

Underfoot, the mud was hard to tug out of; the disturbed water was brackish; twigs floated in it, and sediment rose in clouds.

He splashed the whining insects off, and saw that Galen had slid into the water with him, and that what had been sea was swamp.

It took them over an hour to come ashore properly, and by then the sun was almost setting. They stopped to eat a little and change their clothes, and then started off, stiff with tiredness, walking west.

Galen hurried them on. He knew that if the ship was caught the crew would talk, and if the Watch found out their destination they were in trouble. But more than that, the hunger for Tasceron drove him like a pain; all his blinded senses longed for it, to feel the secrets that were there, the power that might be hidden. Silent, he climbed and scrambled relentlessly over the salt-marsh and through the rough scrub, Carys and Raffi struggling to keep up. No one spoke. The journey became a nightmare of cold, cut hands, breathlessness. For miles they walked into a darkness that seemed to grow thicker before them, even though all seven of the moons rose one by one to form the great Arch, each strange and eerie in its own light, the pearl-pale Karnos, red Pyra, the crescent of Agramon at the zenith.

Then, on a low hill, Galen stopped suddenly. Raffi

sank down, too sore to be glad, doubled over the stitch in his side. It was a while before he lifted his head, breathing deeply.

Below them lay Darkness. A valley of night. Tall spires rose out of it here and there; far, far in the distance strange domes were shadowed with steams and vapors. The blackness was heavy; it stretched as far as he could see. Behind him Carys brushed back her muddy hair; Galen stood upright, saying nothing.

They all knew this was Tasceron.

The Wounded City

16

Tasceron, O Tasceron.
I mourn you, my city.
Your great halls are broken open;
The Darkness has come over you.
Rats eat the finery of your kings.

The Lament for Tasceron

CARYS CRAWLED BACK around the tangle of thorns and sucked a scratched hand. "Useless," she muttered. "They're searching every pack and wagon, looking at everyone's papers. I got close enough to listen. We'll never get in this way."

If anything, Raffi was relieved. He peered through the branches at the city gate. It was a gaunt, dark turret, jutting from the wall, and through the gloom that seemed to seep from it he could make out muffled men and a short line of wagons waiting to pass through.

"Bringing food?" he wondered.

"Probably." Galen stared out, his eyes moving along

the line. Then he glanced up at the walls. The double ramparts of the Evil City were huge and black, smooth, Maker-built. There was no chink or window in them; the great stones stretched away into the eerie dark, and Raffi guessed they ran like that for miles, endless miles. The travelers might walk along them for weeks and not find a breach.

"And if we did it would only be guarded," he muttered aloud.

Galen turned, squatting. In the murk his face was only an edge of shadow, but when he spoke Raffi knew that harsh, determined tone, and felt uneasy.

"I have an idea. It's dangerous, but it seems the only way. These wagons—"

"We're not going to hide in one!" Raffi caught his arm. "Galen, they search them! Stab the flour sacks!"

"Not inside." Galen shook him off irritably. "Underneath."

They were silent. He went on quickly. "They're strong, and small. The axle bars don't look too far apart, and there's a wooden brace between them. We should be able to crawl above it and lie there, just under the planks."

The Wounded City

"It's crazy," Raffi breathed.

"What about your leg?" Carys asked.

The keeper glared at her. "I'll manage. Once we're all through the guard-post, we drop off and meet." He nodded at a tall spire that rose in the darkness. "That building. Or as near to it as we can get. Understand?"

Carys thought, then nodded, reluctant.

"Raffi?"

Shaking his head, he said, "There's got to be a better way . . ."

"There's not." Galen gave him a sharp look. "Trust me, Raffi. I'll take the pack. Let's get nearer."

They worked their way through the scrub to the road, opposite the third wagon in the line. Two men leaned on the front of it, talking. Their voices were clear in the stillness. Far back, a dog barked. Galen touched Carys on the shoulder. She gave one exasperated look at Raffi, then dropped to a crouch and sprinted soundlessly out to the wagon. She slipped under it like a shadow.

"What if they find her?" Raffi whispered, appalled.

"Then they'll find all of us. You next."

The wagons jolted forward; the pack-beasts, mostly

mules, plodding a few weary steps among shouts and one whip-crack. Galen touched Raffi and he ran, stooping low. Halfway there he froze, heart thudding, as the wagoner walked by, kicking the wheels, but the man's back was to him, and in seconds Raffi was ducking underneath, the stink of mule droppings close to his face. Grabbing the front axle, he hauled his chest up over the brace, jamming his feet wide against the planks at the back.

Above him the wagon base was bowed with its load—Galen hadn't thought about that. It lay heavy on his back now, and in a moment of terror he imagined the Watchmen climbing on board and crushing him, and he gripped the greasy axle tight, his cheek lying sideways, the stink of dung in his nostrils.

It was a long time before they moved.

The first jolt almost shook him off; he grabbed tighter, feeling the axle slither and turn. Wrapping himself around the narrow brace, he clung tight, arms and legs aching, hoping he wouldn't slip under it. Then they stopped again and he could loosen his hold.

Gradually the cold seeped into him. After an age of stopping and starting he felt exhausted; on top of the long walk from the ship the strain made his muscles knots of pain, and he was terrified of falling. Splinters of sharp wood jabbed his hands, and the puddles on the muddy roadway splashed his face. Then the wagon stopped again. They were still for so long this time he almost slept; only a wild grab kept him up. After that, a long progress. Looking down, he saw the wheels were crunching in gravel, leaving deep ruts over earlier ones.

They stopped.

"Papers," a voice snarled.

Raffi gripped tight. The man was close. Boots splashed in the grit; he caught the word *barley* and then *a couple of sacks of birds.*

The footsteps moved to the back. Hens squawked right in his ear, and the shaven boards on his back seemed heavier. Gritting his teeth, he waited for the man to climb on, tiny grains of flour and chaff drifting on him in clouds from the opened seams.

The silence was the worst. Axle grease was all over his hands by now, they slipped constantly, and he had to cling on with knees and fingertips, praying to Flain to send him strength to last out. The stiffness of his own muscles tormented him; he sweated, despite the cold, to think he might not be able to unclench them if he needed to run.

A sound, to the left. Cautiously he twisted his head. The boots were back. They stood close by the left front wheel, one up on the rim, the other turned aside. With a hiss of breath, Raffi gripped so tight his hands ached.

The Watchman had dropped something. A coin.

It lay there in the mud. For a terrible second, Raffi stared at it; then the man had bent and was groping for it, his face close to Raffi's, the long straggly hair falling over his eyes. His hand reached under the wheel and touched the coin.

Then he was gone, like a nightmare.

Icy with sweat, Raffi clung on as the wagon began to move, lurching and swaying. The shadow of the gate fell over him; briefly there were paved stones, the hollow echo of hooves in a covered place. Then more mud.

He breathed a prayer. He was in the city.

RAFFI CLUNG TIGHT till the wagon came to a corner and slowed; then he let go and slid down with a thump, unable to stop himself. The street was dim; the wagon rolled noisily over him, its great wheels creaking high on each side. He lay there till it had gone, then picked himself up painfully, his hands so rigid he could hardly open them. Standing upright made him gasp, his knees weak.

"Raffi!"

The hiss was from a doorway; briefly Carys's face showed in a patch of light. "Over here!"

Limping across, he slid in beside her, down to a crouch.

"All right?"

"Half dead." Rubbing his aching arms, he looked up. "Curse Galen to the pit, and all his ideas!"

"It seems to have worked." She sounded amused; looking at her he saw she was filthy, her face smeared with grease. He must look as bad.

"Where now?"

"The building with the spire. It must be close."

They were in a narrow street, evil-smelling, the houses leaning overhead. There was no light, not even from the moons. He wondered if their light ever reached down here, through the blackness of the blighted city. He could glimpse drifts and wraiths of smoke around him, as if the

wind could never blow it away. The vapors rose from
drains and sewers; anyone who lived here in the rotting
city had long forgotten the warmth of the sun. Deep underground, Tasceron was burning. That was its punish-
ment, and for them, its safety.

A rat scuttled down the street. Raffi caught hold of
Carys and they ran close to the walls of the dim buildings, stumbling over rubble and holes. A peculiar low
screech made them stop and look up in terror, and they
saw above the house tops a great dark shape float across
the gloomy gap.

"What was that!"

Carys shook her head. "I daren't think."

When they found it, the building was ruined. A great
hole gaped in the wall; above them the spire crumbled
into darkness.

"Looks like it's going to fall down," Raffi muttered.

"Maybe." Carys glanced around. "Is he here?"

"I don't know." Raffi rubbed his face. He was so tired,
and already the city confused him, the smoke fogging his
sense-lines. Nothing felt clear. He climbed in through the
hole after her.

The Wounded City

It was pitch-black. They edged forward a step.

"Galen?" Raffi whispered. "Galen, are you here?"

The crack of the tinderbox answered him. In a far corner a flame grew; it showed a dark face turning toward them. Carys grinned and took a step in, but Raffi grabbed her, rigid. "It's not him."

The face was filthy. A great burn-mark seared one cheek and, as the man raised himself up, they saw that half of his hair was gone, and the burned scalp was painted with a hideous snake, its great fangs wide. He uncurled himself; stained blankets fell from him; he muttered something and to his right another sleeper groaned and sat up.

Suddenly Raffi saw they were all around him; huddled, uncurling shapes. "Out!" he said. "Get out! Now!"

She was already moving. As he fled he heard shouts; in corners faces rose up and stared at him, grotesque faces without eyes, scarred, skeletal with hunger. Leaping the wall, he flung spell-binds behind him, but it was hard to think; the horror of the uncurling creatures made him race into the darkness heedless, around a corner, down a street, until a shadow stepped out in front of him and grabbed him with both hands.

"Keep still. Keep still!"

"Galen . . ." He was shuddering, breathless.

"I know. They're not following." The keeper dragged him to a dim corner and crouched, while Raffi drew long shuddering breaths, sick with fear, listening to Carys explain. She wasn't afraid, he thought bitterly. And yet he was the one with all the powers. All the defenses.

"Beggars," Galen said grimly. "Or worse. We must get farther in. Right away from the gate. Then we can rest." He looked down at Raffi. "Can you walk?"

Ashamed, Raffi pulled upright. Without a word, Galen turned away.

They traveled down three long streets, then a network of narrow alleys where the rats scrabbled, across wide squares, empty and silent, where only a broken fountain trickled. Deep into the city Galen led them, without direction, looking only for somewhere safe. On each side the doorways were black and sinister. Broken shutters creaked. For Raffi it was a nightmare of weariness and pain; the darkness was foul and in it moved voices and ghosts that strained at his senses, and beyond them was the memory of some great disaster, a horror that seeped and smoked from the very walls and ruins.

Finally, Galen stopped. He searched among the shadows and found a small room in the back of a building; once a house, with a courtyard of black weeds. They searched the place twice and found no one, but Galen wouldn't be satisfied until he had blocked the doorway the best he could with splintered wood. Then, without a fire or bothering to eat, they lay down and slept.

Deep below his ear, deep in the earth, Raffi felt the city smolder and crackle.

17

*Many lies have been told about the fall
of Tasceron. The truth is that whatever
weapon of chaos the Order tried to use
against us blew up in their faces. As will
all their follies.*

Rule of the Watch

It was a crazy plan. As soon as Galen came out with it, I knew we were bound to be caught, so I made sure I went first.

The Watchmen on the gate were thorough, and knew their job. I was out from under that wagon and dragged into the turret in seconds, and it took a great deal of argument to convince them who I was. I knew the passwords, of course, the name of a Watchlord, and I have my agent's insignia on a chain under my clothes. Still, I had to bribe them in the end. And I didn't tell them who Galen was, just that I was working under-cover with two spies, who should be allowed to think no one knew about them.

It worked; we're in, and Galen and Raffi don't know. And yet the gate guards will have sold their knowledge on to someone higher, without doubt.

They're both still asleep. The encounter with that nest of horrors scared Raffi—the shock of it, I suppose. The keeper works him too hard; he can't be ready for all this yet. And on the ship it was Raffi who did the weather-warding.

That unnerved me. It's quite clear the Watch have lied to us, and that makes me angry. The Order do have powers and they're real. It makes me wonder how much else I don't know. The Watch wants all relics—to destroy them, according to our teachers—and yet, I wonder. What if someone high up wants this power for themselves?

This is heresy, of course. If anyone reads it I'll be finished. There was a boy once, in the Watchhouse, I forget his name. We were about seven, and it was in the courtyard, the grim stony place they used to let us play in for ten minutes a day. Three of us were under one coat for warmth. He said, this boy, that his grandfather had told him that the Makers were real men, and that their power was enormous. And that he thought the Watch had been wrong to kill so many of the Order.

Someone must have reported what he said, because a week later he was taken away, and he never came back. Like a lot of others . . .

"I DIDN'T KNOW you could write."

Carys closed the journal with a gasp, and spun around. Galen was sitting up against the wall, watching her. For a moment she was lost for an answer. Then Watchtraining surged up in her; she shook her head and laughed. "You scared me!"

"I'm sorry."

She slipped the journal into her bag. "My mother taught me, a long time ago. I don't know how she learned— probably with one of the Order. There were many keepers when she was young."

"Indeed there were." Galen frowned, rubbing his stubbly chin. "But it seemed to be in a language strange to me."

For a moment she looked at him. Then she said, "It's in code."

"Code?"

"I made it up myself. In case the Watch should ever get hold of it. It's the story of my search."

"Then we're in there—the boy and I?"

"Only briefly." She shook her head. "I've changed your names. No one would ever be able to read it."

"I hope not." He pulled the pack over and began to rummage inside. "They say the Watch have men skilled in codes and secret signs. If they caught you with it they'd force you to explain it."

She nodded. "You mean get rid of it."

He passed her some bread. "It would be wise."

Wanting to change the subject, she said, "Shall we wake Raffi?"

"No. Let him sleep."

They ate in silence, listening. A long way off something banged, and once Carys thought she heard voices, but the city was as dark and silent as before, the only sound a faint rushing, as if water ran nearby. She knew it must be late in the day, but outside the blocked doorway the blackness still hung.

"Does it ever get light here?"

The Wounded City

Galen shook his head. In the tiny candle flame his hawk-face looked tired and drawn; he tugged the string out of his hair and raked his fingers through it. "Not since the Destruction."

"What happened?" she asked, chewing the hard bread.

"You know. Or you ought to."

"Tell me again." She did know, but she was curious to hear how the Order told the story.

Galen gave her a hard look. Then he said, "The Order had its most holy sites here. Somewhere in the city, buried deep under layers of other buildings, were the secret places, the houses of the Makers. The House of Trees, the Nemeta, the Hall of the Slain. Where exactly they were is not known now. The Emperor's palace was here too. In the last hours of the siege, when men were fighting in the streets and the Emperor knew the war was lost, it's said he sent a message to Mardoc Archkeeper, to warn him. That was late on Pyrasnight, about eight o'clock. Two hours later the palace fell. The Emperor was killed at the Phoenix Gate—you know about that?"

She nodded, silent. The Emperor had been killed by

accident, by some fool of a Watchsergeant. The Watch-lords had thrown the man into the demon-pit at Maar in their fury. They had wanted the Emperor alive.

"And then," Galen went on, his voice dropping, "late in the night, with the hordes of the Watch loot-ing and spoiling the city, there was a great trembling of the ground. Buildings fell. Whole districts crumbled. Fires erupted underground. And from somewhere deep among the alleys and courts of the old palace, the Dark-ness came. They say it spread like ink over a map, blot-ting out the moons and stars, filling alleys, doorways, oozing out from cellars and pits and manholes in the streets, up sewers and drains.

"What it was, how it was released, no one knows now, or whether it was meant to happen. So much is lost, Carys!" He sighed, scratching his cheek. "The Arch-keeper escaped. He was caught three months later and died under torture, but I don't believe he told them where the Houses were. If he had, they'd be in ruins, and the Watch would be gloating. They want all the power they can get." He spat, savagely, to one side.

Carys was silent. She took some more bread. "The

Watch say Mardoc tried to bring the Makers back. That he had some relic which was so powerful that its explosion would make the city burn forever."

"They would!" Galen watched Raffi stir and roll over. "But Mardoc got out. Something that big would have killed him."

"And what about the Crow?"

She said it slowly, deliberately. Raffi, half awake, stared at her in astonishment; Galen slid his eyes to her.

"What about him?" he asked, after a cold moment.

Carys smiled, but Raffi knew she was uneasy. "All right. I suppose I should tell you. I listened at Lerin's door."

Galen's hand clutched his stick; for a moment Raffi thought he would use it on her and scrambled up, gasping, "No!" but Carys only laughed scornfully. "I'm not your scholar, Galen. Don't think you can beat me into silence."

He stared at her, and Raffi caught the strange taints of anger and despair that wreathed him. Finally, in a voice choked with wrath, he said, "How much did you hear?"

"That the Crow is here in Tasceron. That you'd had messages. That you thought, if you could find him, he could destroy the Watch."

She leaned forward, her hair glossy in the flame light. "That was all. I'm sorry, Galen, but I had to know what was happening! I'm here to find my father, and I don't know where to start. But the Crow! With him we could do anything!"

The silence was terrible. Raffi pulled the blanket around himself and rubbed his face nervously with a filthy hand. Galen sat absolutely still, watching Carys with a bitter stare that made her hand creep toward the crossbow. When he spoke his voice was hoarse. "Never spy on me again, girl. Never."

The threat was cold, and real. Chilled, she nodded. It took all her courage to say, "I want to stay with you. I want to help."

But Galen got up abruptly. Taking his stick, he flung the wood from the doorway. "Stay here. I'll be back."

"Where are you going?" Raffi asked.

"Out!" The keeper stared at him grimly. "To breathe!"

When he was gone, they both relaxed. Raffi drank

some water from the flask and passed it across; kneeling up, he felt for the bread in the pack.

"Was I wrong to tell him?" Carys asked quietly.

He shrugged. "I don't know. We'd have had to explain to you soon, I suppose. And he would have found out. He's a keeper."

"He hadn't yet," she said drily.

Raffi glanced at her, then away. "How could you listen at the door, Carys! We thought we could trust you!"

Looking down at the flask, she said, "You can. Of course you can."

GALEN WAS A LONG time away. When he finally came back he said nothing about Carys or the Crow. Crouching, he crammed the blankets into the pack. "There's a fountain not far from here, still running. The water's tainted, but drinkable. And you can wash."

His own hair was wet and his face clean.

"Then what?" Carys asked.

He gave her a bitter glare. "You'll find out."

They crossed a maze of small lanes, following the

splashing sound, then turned into an open space among tall buildings, whose tops were lost in dark smoke. The fountain was astonishingly hot, the water steaming from spouts and holes among stones that had once been white, but were now streaked with soot. Carys and Raffi drank and washed their arms and faces, while Galen kept watch, eyeing the narrow streets intently. The water was pungent and sour, despite the green lichens that grew out of it.

When they'd finished and were pulling their coats on, Galen said, "Now listen to me. We're making for the old citadel and the ruins of the palace. They should be somewhere to the south, deep within the city. It may take us days. The farther in we go, the more dangerous it will be. Watchpatrols for sure, but I suspect they'll keep to the wider streets. Even the Watch will be wary of the others here."

"Is there anyone?" Carys muttered, looking at the dim openings.

"Don't be a fool. There are thieves, footpads, murderers, all the dregs of the world. And madmen—this place is haunted by them. Other creatures too—beasts swollen and warped by the great Destruction, made savage by the dark. It's not called the Evil City for nothing."

Carys pulled a face, then checked her crossbow. Galen drew Raffi aside. "Sense-lines. As many as you can."

Raffi nodded unhappily. "The trouble is, the buildings—or the dark—something's confusing me. There are too many echoes here."

"Try! We're depending on you now!"

Carys was watching them. Galen picked up the pack and slung it on. Then he stood upright, a tall shadow in the steamy gloom. "Keep close. And keep silent."

They set off into a narrow alley that stank of decay and skeats—the packs of small wild dogs Raffi had seen once before. Halfway down, it was blocked with fallen timbers; crawling under these they found themselves at a crossroads. Six black lanes led away into gloom like the spokes of a wheel. Everything was silent.

With a quick glance at Raffi, Galen strode into the farthest left. A very quick glance. But Carys had seen it.

Through the next few hours, she came to see that it was Raffi who was leading them. Sensing direction in the eternal gloom of Tasceron was almost impossible—there

were no moons and no sunrise, and the labyrinth of buildings was intricate and unknown. But a keeper's soul was
linked with the earth, deep with stone and tree and soil,
and they felt the magnetic lines deep inside themselves.
Or so they said. So Raffi knew where the south was. But
did Galen? Once, when he walked straight past a turning
and Raffi had to call him back, she saw something in his
face that puzzled and chilled her. A wretchedness. Almost
despair.

There was no time to think about it. They soon found
that Tasceron was inhabited. Coming around a bend,
they heard voices, and pressing back quickly into shadow,
they watched a group of armed men cross between the
houses. They wore remnants of armor, ill-patched and
rusted; some covered with ragged surcoats and jerkins of
what looked like skeat fur. Two wore helmets.

These were the Watch. Close up, they were a ragged
rabble, but they moved fast, with discipline; their swords
were bright and when Raffi saw the grim knot of prisoners they dragged behind, tied wrist and waist, he shivered
and pressed back into the doorway.

For a long time the tramp of feet echoed in the ruins. Finally Galen said, "We were lucky they didn't have hounds."

After that they moved more carefully. The maze of dark courts and tunnels bewildered Carys; she knew she'd never find her way back. They walked for hours; the world shrank to brick, rubble, stairs, the sad remnants of gardens, blackened and fire-scarred. Once they heard a great roaring far off and stood rigid, but it didn't come again. Often rats scattered among the broken houses; clouds of biting insects infested some areas, and everywhere the owls hooted: great sooty-gray owls that swooped down the murky alleys silently.

Twice they crossed rivers on bridges that were crumbling to pieces, and between their feet they saw the black oily water racing below the holes. At the second bridge something leaped out and caught hold of Raffi, mumbling snarling words; Galen gave it a swift blow with his staff and it scuttled, crouched low, into the dark.

They ran then, till they were clear of the place.

"What was that!" Carys gasped.

Galen scowled her into silence, listening to their own echoes, endlessly pattering.

"Are you all right?" she whispered to Raffi.

He nodded wearily. "What a place. Can the Crow really be here?"

But Galen was gone, and they hurried after him.

Later they paused briefly to eat, but soon moved on, always keeping to the clearer streets if they could. Some alleys were so evil-smelling, so filled with stench and black mist, that Galen avoided them, despite the time lost.

Then, under one overhanging house, Carys paused. Her boots were coated with slimy weed, making her slip; she scraped it off hastily. Darkness closed over her. She glanced up and stared, paralyzed with astonishment. The thing was black, huge and winged. Its evil face had tiny eyes; hooked talons slashed at her.

"Get down!"

Galen's yell made her drop. With a whistle of stinking breath the thing swooped over her, its call eerie and wild. Rolling, she jabbed a bolt into the bow. The thing flew back, its claws raked her face; she kicked aside and fired. The creature shrieked, a blot of darkness against the gloom.

"Run!" Galen was yelling. "There are more!"

The Wounded City

Scrambling up, she limped after him, fumbling for another bolt, leaping a shattered wall. Looking up made her skin crawl. The sky was infested with the things; they dropped noiselessly, flapping, screeching, so fast she could hardly make them out.

Ahead, the street turned a corner. Racing around it, she caught up with Raffi, ducking with a yell as one of the things screamed low, its claws snatching at her hair. Then she slammed into a wall, hands flat. Turning, she slid to a crouch, jerking up the bow, hearing Galen yell with fury.

The alley was a dead end.

They were trapped.

18

Out of Darkness shall come Light.
Pilgrims shall walk on the Roads of
the Sky.

Apocalypse of Tamar

RAFFI BUCKLED AGAINST THE WALL next to Carys. She had her bow up; for a second he saw the bolt, then it was gone. But there was so much screeching overhead he couldn't tell if any of the things had been hurt.

Galen fell beside him, ducking, arms over head. "Lights!" he yelled. "Mind-lights!"

Raffi was appalled. "I can't!"

"TRY!"

He tried. He searched for his inner eye; it was buried deep in his mind, closed tight. Opening it took an age; dimly, far off, he heard the shrieks of the attack-

251

ing beasts and Carys yelling with anger. Then he saw a tiny purple light and caught hold of it, made it swell and brighten. It was in the darkness before him, wobbling, expanding; now it was glowing and crackling, and briefly he saw Galen turn, and Carys's eyes wide in amazement. The pale globe pulsed in the alley, it gleamed on the black wings that drove straight at him. He leaped back, cracked his head on the wall, and staggered, half stunned.

The globe popped like a soap bubble.

Darkness swallowed them; the sky shrieked.

"Do something!" Carys was crouched over Raffi, looking up, her face cut. "You're the keeper, Galen!" she yelled, furious. "Do something!"

Their eyes met. In that instant she knew, without doubt, that there was nothing he could do. He was powerless.

Then he stood up recklessly, stepping out from the wall.

At once the light came. It came suddenly, a great slot of it streaming out, bright yellow light, the first light they had seen for days, and it dazzled them as it swung open across the filthy alley, spilling on black walls and dead moss, and over Galen, as he spun around, his face sharp with thrown shadow. Above it the black night-things screamed in rage, flashes of talon and wing. Then they swooped and were gone.

Carefully, in the sudden hush, Carys picked herself up. Raffi followed, one hand flat against the wall.

"Am I interrupting you?" a dry voice asked from the doorway.

None of them answered. The man gave a strange bark of laughter and stepped out, and Raffi forgot the pain in his head.

Because it wasn't a man. It was a Sekoi.

It was a little taller than Galen, and thin, with the starved look they had. A long, seven-fingered hand held the lantern up. On its sharp face a tribe mark zigzagged under one eye; the short fur was a brindled gray. It wore old patched clothes of green and brown.

"Come inside," it said. "Come inside."

After a second Carys obeyed; the others came behind her and the Sekoi bolted the door.

Galen shook off his shock. "We should thank you," he murmured.

"Indeed you should. You owe me your lives, keeper."
It pointed a thin finger at Galen's chest and smiled.

Galen growled. "What makes you think . . ."

The Sekoi put its small mouth very close to Galen's ear
and whispered solemnly, "An owl told me." Its eyes were
bright; a strange purr of amusement came from its throat.
Galen looked disgusted.

"What were those things?" Carys wiped the blood
from her cheek.

"We call them draxi." The creature looked at her
closely. "Half bird, half beast. Hideous and dangerous—
one of Kest's mistakes. But they don't like light."

"Useful to know," she muttered.

Swinging the lamp, the Sekoi turned. "Up now."

They were in a tiny dim hall, with a spiral staircase in
one corner. The creature ran up quickly and they hurried
after it, the lantern light bouncing off the walls ahead.
After five minutes they were breathless and their legs felt
like lead; Galen was limping heavily. Finally, turning a
corner, they found the Sekoi waiting for them, leaning
against the wall biting its nails.

It smiled kindly. "Tired? A long way to go yet."

The Wounded City

"To where?" Carys demanded.

"Safety." It picked up its lantern. "Careful now. There are holes."

It led them through an arch to an uneven chamber, where wooden planking seemed to have been laid over a sloping, swelling floor. The roof above was so low they had to crawl. Raffi guessed that the floor itself was the roof of some vault or dome below; once he put his hand through a hole and felt nothing but emptiness. The dust was so thick that he made handprints in it, and the lantern, hanging around the Sekoi's neck, threw wild, swinging shadows.

They crossed three vaults like this, each one more cramped. In the last the roof scraped their backs. Galen slithered to a halt. "Where are you taking us?" he growled.

Ahead, they caught the Sekoi's grin in a swing of the lantern.

"Safety lies in secrecy, keeper. You know that." It turned and crawled on. Galen gripped his stick and swore.

Finally the Sekoi came to a tiny door in the wall and opened it. "If you fear heights," its voice said, rather muffled, "don't look down."

Coming through the door and straightening up with relief, Raffi found himself on a curved balcony; a rail was to his left, and to his right a wall that glinted here and there. He saw remnants of faces, giant hands, gold, scarlet, and blue. Galen caught the Sekoi's arm roughly.

"What are these?" His voice echoed, hissing in far distances.

Impatiently the Sekoi glared at him, then held the lantern up. "Mosaics. Images. Of the Star-people. The ones you call the Makers. This, look, is Flain."

Galen, astonished, made the gesture of peace; Raffi did the same. In the weak light the enormous face of a man gazed down sternly at them, pieced together from marble, porphyry, precious stones. Parts of it had been hacked out. Staring at the vast eyes, all at once Raffi sensed echoes; lost sense-lines. Turning, he caught hold of the rail and leaned over.

"Be careful!" the Sekoi hissed.

The darkness was immense. A gust of wind blew against him; he glimpsed appalling distances, the floor so far below that he gripped the rail tight with cold fingers, feeling the world swing away under him. Dizzy, he hung on.

The Wounded City

They were above some vast empty place, once a temple. The wind howled through its shattered windows. In the darkness he made out glimpses of pillars, fallen altars, smashed statues. Awed, Raffi gazed down, feeling Galen beside him.

"One of ours."

"Once." The keeper was chilled; the destruction filled him with bitterness.

"Hurry now." The Sekoi tapped their backs. "And keep away from the rail. It breaks."

Tiny in the immense curve of the dome, they followed the star of the lantern, clinging flat to the wall in places where the rail had gone and only emptiness hung. Once, far down in that blackness, something small clattered. The Sekoi whipped its coat over the light; breathless, they waited in the pitch dark.

"Rats," Carys breathed finally.

The Sekoi sniffed. "Maybe," it said quietly.

They went on more carefully. Another endless set of stairs, this time between two tight walls. At the top, the Sekoi blew out the lantern.

"What are you doing!" Galen roared from the dark.

They heard a door unlocking. A slot opened in the wall, and to their immense astonishment, sunlight blinded them. With a yell of delight Carys jumped down into it, onto the broad expanse of a roof that spread far and flat into the sky. The sun shone; faint clouds drifted. It was about three o'clock in the afternoon, and one of the moons hung high and still like a smudge of chalk dust.

"We're above the Darkness!" Raffi stepped down, awed.

The air was clean and cold. Far, far off, the mountains were green in the sun. All the colors exhilarated Raffi; he ran to the parapet and gazed down. Below him, he saw only the smoke and darkness of Tasceron; a black vapor, out of which rose spires and domes, high roofs, spindly towers, and joining them all, a fantastic rickety structure of ladders and bridges, walkways, ropes, high in the sky.

"What is this?" Galen asked.

"The way the Sekoi travel. None of us likes the Darkness, keeper, any more than you. So we live up here, when we come to the city. Which is not often." It turned graciously. "My tribe built this. At the moment I'm the only one here."

On the roof was a scatter of tents, patched and sewn, and some bigger huts, made from wood nailed inexpertly together. The Sekoi took them to the nearest, went in, and tossed out some cushions.

"Be comfortable," it said, and disappeared inside.

Suddenly worn out, Raffi crumpled onto the silk and lay back in luxury, closing his eyes in the sun's warmth. Galen sat beside him, easing his sore leg. Carys watched.

The keeper looked at her; she felt awkward and uneasy. At last she muttered, "You should have told me."

Raffi opened his eyes. "Told you what?"

"Not you. Him."

Galen's eyes were black, like a bird's; he eased the green and jet crystals from inside his coat and ran his fingers over them. "Nothing to do with you," he said fiercely.

Raffi sat up. Anxious, he watched them both.

"Of course it is," she snapped. "We're in this together. If I'd known you'd lost all . . ."

His glare stopped her. Raffi looked away. "When did you find out?" Galen murmured.

"Down there. In the alley. Though I'd thought before that something was wrong." She kept her eyes on Galen. "No wonder you want so much to find the Crow."

Before he could answer, the Sekoi was back, carrying a great platter of fruit. "This is all my people eat," it said, "so it will have to do."

"Where did you get it?" Raffi asked, taking a dew-apple.

"There are ways. Some I brought with me. There are places to buy in the city, but they're brief, furtive, dirty. Knife-in-the-back. Not safe."

Carys took some fruit and ate it hungrily; Galen was slower, and silent. There was clean water to drink, flavored by a sweet sugar that made Raffi realize his thirst.

It was only when the plate was empty that the Sekoi said, "And how is dear Alberic?"

Galen looked up. "How do you know so much about us?"

It purred again, the long fingers brushing its neck-fur.

The Wounded City

"The Order have many secrets, keeper; so do we. Certainly I knew Alberic would send someone after me. He knew I would bring his gold here. And as I said, the owls told me you were in the district." It smirked, showing small sharp teeth. "I gather I'm not your main interest though. Did I just hear the word *Crow*?"

Galen gave Carys a vicious stare. "It appears you did."

The Sekoi shook its head sadly. "You're foolish, keeper, ever to have come here. Nothing of the Makers is left. We'd know."

Raffi looked at Galen, but the keeper's face was hard. "I think you're wrong. Tomorrow, I want you to take us where we might find some of the Order."

The Sekoi scratched the fur over one eye. "The Order!"

"There must be someone left."

It seemed to be thinking. "Maybe. It will be dangerous."

"Good." Morosely Galen watched the sun sink into a red cloud. "All the better."

Journal of Carys Arrin
Date unknown

Galen meditates. For hours. His prayers are all that keep him going. I don't feel glad that I found out about this. It makes things easier for me, and explains a lot, but . . .

Well, I feel sorry for him.

I must be getting soft.

19

*You will find that the Sekoi can often
be bought—their greed for gold is well
known. What they do with it and where
they hide it have never been discovered.
Their storytelling is some form of
hypnosis and may affect the unwary.
Keep away from them. They are of no
importance.*

Rule of the Watch

WHEN RAFFI WOKE, the Sekoi was sitting next to him, its long hands curled under its chin. "At last," it said. "You're awake."

Carys was pacing impatiently, Galen saying the morning litany cross-legged in one corner of the roof. As he stood up, the Sekoi said, "I'm afraid I have no breakfast for you. Should we leave now?"

"Wait." Galen took the last of Lerin's food from the pack and shared it around. The Sekoi took a small piece of cheese and nibbled it daintily, pulling a few faces. It swallowed, bravely.

"Exquisite."

"Stale," Raffi muttered.

"Really?" The creature's fur was fine over its face; Raffi noticed the yellow brightness of its eyes. Abruptly it said, "I should tell you that the Watch know you're here."

Galen almost choked. "Here?"

"In the city."

"How?" Raffi gasped.

"Someone must have told them."

"But no one's seen us!"

The Sekoi purred, amused. "Don't be fooled, small scholar. Many will have seen you. You may not have seen them. The city is full of eyes and spies. I've heard there are patrols out looking for you."

Galen looked bleak. He ran a hand through his black hair. Carys glanced away. Her heart was thudding but she kept calm. It had to be the Watchmen at the gate. Rapidly she thought it out. Now someone higher up knew she was here—but not who the others were; not yet. This would make it harder, though. Everywhere would be watched.

As if it read her thoughts, the Sekoi stood and stretched

lazily. "But no patrols where we go, masters." It turned and waved a web of fingers airily. "We walk in the sky."

The sun glittered on the highest tips of the city, rising from the dark mists below. The Sekoi led them to a corner of the roof and leaped elegantly over a narrow gap to a small bridge that swayed under its weight. Raffi followed; clutching the rope to hold himself, he glanced down and saw the gap between the roofs was filled to the brim with the swirling smoke. Just as well, he thought, imagining how high up they were.

"Move!" Galen yelled. "Hurry up."

Raffi frowned. The Relic Master's temper was getting worse the farther they went.

ALL MORNING THEY FOLLOWED the Sekoi over the intricate sky-road. It was cobbled together: a chain of bridges, rope-swings, planks, and stairway on stairway of trembling, wind-battered steps, around precarious domes and steeples, nested on by birds, stained by rain and the stench from the murk below. They climbed among chimneys, broken tiles, balustrades and balconies, belfries where the cracked bells still hung, filthy with bird droppings, silent since the city's fall. It was cold up here, exhilarating; Raffi found himself almost happy, just being in the sun again. He could see here, he knew where he was. He sent sense-lines spinning into the clouds.

Finally though, he saw the road was running out. Fewer and fewer buildings pierced the dark, and some of the aerial stairways were broken. Twice they had to turn back. When the Sekoi stopped, on the parapet of a small dome, it helped Raffi up with a furred hand.

"Not dizzy?"

He shook his head. "Though I would be if I could see the ground."

"Ah." The creature leaned out and looked down. "So even Darkness has its uses. Worthy of your Litany, that idea." It glanced back at Galen. "I wonder if that's true of all darkness."

Raffi stared at the Sekoi, but it winked at him and said no more. After a moment Raffi said, "You didn't tell us your name."

"We don't tell our names, little scholar. Not to out-siders." It tapped the zigzag mark under its eye. "That's my name. It would just sound like a snarl to you. Didn't teach you much about us, did he?"

"The Sekoi hate water and the dark," Raffi quoted quickly. "They imperil their souls with riches; they tell intricate lies."

The creature winced. "I see." It made a small face. "Well, it's accurate. Gold is precious to us. The sorrows of Kest come to everyone, even us, who were here before the Starmen. But now, I'm afraid, this is as far as we go. Come and see."

Without waiting for the others, it walked around the dome, balancing easily on a narrow flaking ledge of stone, putting one foot delicately before the other. Raffi inched after it, arms wide, holding on to moldings and carved faces that crumbled in his hands. Breathless, the wind plucking at him, he sidled around to a wider part and found the Sekoi sitting, its legs dangling over the abyss.

"There," it said softly. "The great wound."

Before them, as far as they could see, the Darkness lay unbroken. Remote in the distance, the sun caught the tops of other towers, but the heart of the city was black and drowned, with nothing left high enough to pierce the eternal murk. Here the Darkness was vast; it steamed and churned, almost thick enough to walk on.

"So we go back down, then?" Carys said. She had come around silently; now she watched Galen balance, the staff strapped to his back.

"Down and down," the Sekoi said mournfully. "That is, if you still want to."

"We do," the keeper said at once.

"Pity. All the dangers lie down there."

"That's nothing to me," Galen growled.

The Sekoi raised an eyebrow at Raffi. "If you say so."

A door in the dome led them to a stair, and they followed it down. After only minutes the light faded away; by the time they'd passed the third cracked window, darkness was back around them, and the Sekoi had to light its lantern and hold it up. Rats scattered all down the stairs.

Raffi felt his heart sink back into gloom. The sense-lines dimmed. From somewhere down below, the stench of something rotting made him retch. At the bottom of the stairs the Sekoi put the lantern out and hid it. Following through twists and turns of walls, they found themselves in a ruined courtyard. Picking its way through broken pillars and the leaning column of a sundial, the Sekoi paused under an archway. Beyond it the alley was black.

"Where now?" Galen muttered.

The creature eyed him. Then it said, "A few streets away is a story-house. A place where my people gather. We may find someone there who can help. Remember, keep silent."

They moved close together. After the sunlight above, Raffi felt he had gone blind. But gradually walls re-emerged from the gloom, dim outlines. They walked silently down a long street past what had once been shops; now they were drafty holes where rubbish gusted. The street felt cobbled, narrow between the high walls of grim buildings; a shutter banging in the silence; a fountain clotted with dead leaves.

Halfway down the Sekoi turned right, into a blacker crack; a strange archway spanned the entrance and under it Raffi caught a few words carved beautifully in stone: "Street of the Arch," still clear after centuries.

Galen had stopped; he made a rapt sign with his hand. "Look there, Raffi."

Above the street name was a niche with the remains of a statue. Fragments now, but Raffi knew in an instant what it had been: Soren, her arms full of flowers. A carved lily was still perfect in the stone.

"Hurry," the Sekoi hissed from the dark.

Moving after it, Raffi tried to imagine the city as it had been once, filled with sunlight, full of shining statues of the Makers, its fountains rippling pure water, its streets thronged with pilgrims. For a moment he believed it, but it made the Darkness seem worse.

He almost walked past the others; Carys caught him. They were gathered in a narrow doorway. The Sekoi knocked twice, varying the pattern. Then it knocked again, four times.

They waited, nervous, in the inky street. Glancing back, Carys knew if a patrol was watching them it would be impossible to see. She fought off the sudden panicky thought and turned back.

Without a sound, a small grille in the door had opened. The Sekoi muttered a few sounds into it. Seconds later, the door was unlocked.

They never saw the doorkeeper. The Sekoi hustled

them in down a lightless passage; the door locked behind them as they crossed a courtyard to an inner door. The Sekoi turned, blocking the way. "It's best if you say nothing. They won't speak to you anyway. Sit and watch. Try not to listen."

With that strange remark they went in. The room was small, and lit with green candles that gave a wonderful light. To Raffi's joy, it was full of Sekoi; about a dozen of the creatures, lounging on cushions around a fire. They all turned and looked as the strangers came in; then, as one, they looked away again.

"Sit down," the Sekoi whispered. There were empty cushions in a corner; Carys perched on one, knees up. The storyteller, a female Sekoi sitting by the fire, did not pause; it went on speaking in their language of strange purring consonants, one hand moving as it talked, throwing deft shadows.

Fascinated, Raffi watched. He had never seen so many of them; he noticed the different colors and patterns of their fur, the small tribemarks. There were no young ones, though. No children. Each had an absorbed look, as if they dreamed or were in some trance as they listened, and they took not the slightest notice of the travelers.

Finally, the story came to an end. There was no applause, just silence, and then the creatures talked excitedly to one another.

"Why are they ignoring us?" Carys asked, annoyed.

The Sekoi smiled. "My people are honest. If the Watch question them they can say they've talked to no keeper, no Starmen."

It uncurled itself and crossed the room and, taking the storyteller by the arm, began to whisper.

Galen fidgeted. "Are we safe here? How does it feel?"

"There's nothing. I can't read Sekoi."

"I could." The keeper's hawk-face darkened. "But then, they're usually safe. They despise most Starmen, especially the Watch. But not the Order."

"Why call us Starmen?" Carys asked.

"Because the Makers came from the sky. The Sekoi say they watched them come. They have stories about it." He laughed harshly. "They have stories about everything."

Behind the quiet talk another teller had begun; an old-looking Sekoi mumbling almost to itself. As he sat there, Raffi felt the pattern of words; at first they meant nothing to him, but as Galen and Carys talked, their voices faded out and the room rippled, as if it were an image in water. He closed his eyes and opened them, but the rippling went on; he turned to speak to Galen about it but the keeper had gone; all around him was a dark hillside under the stars, brilliantly frosty, and the seven moons beyond, making the Ring.

Standing there, Raffi shivered in the cold, feeling his fur thicken, seeing the night in new colors, colors that had no words but Sekoi words, and he said them to himself, quietly delighted.

In the sky, a light moved. It was a star that grew; it came closer to him, and the hum and glitter of it shook the frosted tops of the trees, and he saw how vast the stars were. It came down and landed. The whole world shook with its weight.

The star opened and the man walked out. Flain was tall and his hair was long and bright. But the sight of him made the fur on Raffi's neck shiver; he rubbed at it and someone's hand caught his and said, "Raffi! Raffi!"

Galen was crouched over him. Behind, the Sekoi was smiling. "I told you not to listen," it purred.

Galen glared at it. "Is he all right?"

"Perfectly. Aren't you?"

Raffi nodded, confused. He looked over, but the story-teller mumbled on, and now the words were impossible to understand.

"Listen," the Sekoi said. "I've been advised that you should try the Street of the Wool-Carders. Apparently there may be a contact there. We should look for the name Anteus."

Galen nodded. "Where is that?"

"Not too far. But near a Watchtower. I could show you."

Galen looked at it curiously. "Why are you helping us?"

The Sekoi narrowed its yellow eyes. "Because the Watch think we're worthless animals." It grinned. "And in memory of our mutual friend, Alberic."

"Have you still got his gold?" Raffi asked.

The Sekoi drew itself up, affronted. "My gold. He should pay his storytellers."

Carys laughed. She wished she knew where the Sekoi hoard was. That would be useful information. But the Crow was better.

The Wounded City

Back out in the black city, they headed for the Street of the Wool-Carders. All the streets seemed the same, but, crossing one huge empty square, Raffi sensed the space all around him, and eyes at his back. Spinning around, he saw only darkness.

When he told Carys, she took the crossbow off her shoulder and loaded it. "I've been afraid of that."

"If only I could sense something clear!"

"I thought keepers were good at that."

"Not here."

The street, when they found it, was very short and bounded by a low wall with some sort of neglected garden on the other side; dead branches snapped under their feet. They walked up and down it twice, but there were no houses, no doors.

Galen leaned on his stick. "So much for the Sekoi," he snarled bitterly.

The creature rubbed its fur thoughtfully. "We may be looking for the wrong thing."

"How?"

"Does not your Order have secrets, keeper? Signs, symbols? Things not known by outsiders?"

Galen straightened. "Raffi. Go with him. Search every inch of this wall. Girl, come with me."

In the dimness they had to peer at the bricks, feel with fingertips. Halfway down Raffi stopped. "This is it," he breathed.

The Sekoi stared curiously at the mess of scratches. "It means nothing."

"Yes it does." He turned. "Galen!"

The keeper came at a run, shoving him aside. "Good, Raffi! Good!"

On the wall was a broken inscription plaque, with the words ". . . memory of Anteus, who . . ." all that re-mained. But under that were new scratches, strange and meaningless. Galen's fingers outlined them eagerly. A tiny bee, a circle of six dots and another inside, a group of enigmatic slashes and squiggles. Carys tried to get closer. "What does it say?" she hissed.

Galen glanced at her. Then he said to the Sekoi, "Where's the place called the Pyramid?"

It looked surprised. "An hour's walk south. Why?"

"That's where we go."

All the way there Galen said nothing else, but Raffi

could feel the pain in him, the desperate rising hope. Some of the way they ran, as time was running out; even Carys felt eyes on her, the scurrying of shapes in the shadows. She constantly glanced behind her at the darkest corners. Once she laughed at herself—she was the Watch, after all—but in this place everything seemed full of doubt. She knew she was beginning to look like an outlaw, to think like one. She had almost forgotten herself, and the knowledge shook her.

Overhead the draxi flapped, looming out of fog; Raffi glanced up at them with a shudder.

Crouched under walls, against buildings, they ran deeper and deeper into Tasceron's heart. Finally the Sekoi stopped by a smooth sloping wall. "Well, keeper," it said, breathless. "Your Pyramid."

The top was lost in gloom. They walked around it. Four walls, with no opening. It was blank and smooth.

"Now what?" Carys muttered.

Galen put both hands on the brickwork. He began to speak, words that not even Raffi knew—fierce, secret sounds—so that Carys stared and the Sekoi put its long hands together and chewed its nails nervously.

The spell ended. But nothing moved.

In a rage of fury, Galen slammed his hands against the wall, kicked it, beat at it. He moaned and cursed, his voice an agony in the silence. It chilled them all. For a moment Raffi wondered if Galen's mind had gone. Then Galen turned. He looked over Raffi's shoulder into the dark and there was a look on his haggard face that terrified them.

But all he said was, "We're going to have to improve your sense-lines, boy."

Carys spun around.

The Sekoi snarled.

Behind them, a row of armed men was waiting in the gloom.

20

There will be one who will return from the black pit.
   And yet he will not be the one who went.

Apocalypse of Tamar

"MY NAME IS NOT FOR YOU YET," the old man said. He nodded to the nearest swordsman. "Search the pack."

They were inside the Pyramid, though Raffi still wasn't sure how it had opened. The scuffle in the street had been brief; the men had dragged them in and flung them down there in a heap. The Sekoi had a torn ear, and Carys's crossbow was in a swordsman's hand.

Now Raffi watched in fury as the pack was tugged open; one by one their clothes were tossed out, the water flask, the tinderbox. Finally the relic bag. The swordsman tossed it to the old man, who held it a moment.

"What might be in here?"

Galen was silent. Raffi's heart thumped.

The old man smiled. His face was small and narrow, his hair gray as ash, clipped short. He wore black gloves. Opening the bag, he took out the relics, laying them carefully on the table. "A device for far-seeing! I've heard of such a thing."

He laid the Maker-gifts in a row, and Carys stared at them. She had no idea what most of them were: a green tube, a box with buttons on it, a flimsy see-through cube. The old man's hand paused in the bag. Raffi felt a sharp tingle of emotion from him, a shock of surprise. Then the black glove came out; it held the glass ball they had found long ago on the island.

"What's this?" The old man looked up intently. "Where did you get this?"

Galen's voice was grim. "I've never seen it before."

The old man stared at him for a moment, then he sat on a wooden bench. "Shean," he said after a little while. "My name is Pieter Shean. I'm a Relic Master of the Order of keepers, as you are, Galen Harn."

Galen's face didn't change. "Prove it."

The Wounded City

Shean shook his head. "What harm have they done us, my friend! But hear this." He said nothing, but Galen's eyes widened briefly; he sat upright and Raffi felt the sudden surge of joy in him.

"I have not heard a voice in my mind these three months," Galen muttered hoarsely.

"I know it. I feel all the pain of it." The old man nodded to the swordsmen. "All is well. Go back out."

The men went. One of them grinned at Carys and handed back her crossbow with a flourish. Annoyed, she snatched it. He wouldn't smile if he knew who she was. Then she squashed the thought. This Shean hadn't lost his power. She'd have to be careful. And take a good look around.

The old man waved them to seats. "I'm sorry for your treatment. My men needed to be sure you weren't Watchspies. Of you, keeper, I'm sure, and your boy, and the Sekoi have rarely harmed us. But who is this girl?"

"Carys Arrin." Galen kept her quiet with a look. "We met her far from here, on the downs in our own country. The Watch took her father."

Shean studied her carefully. "Did they? When?"

"Months ago," she muttered. "I thought they might be bringing him here."

"I know of no prisoners brought from so far. It would be more likely they would take him to Arnk, or the Pits at Maar." He turned to Galen. "Are you sure of her? The Watch have so many spies."

Galen was silent. Then he said, "I know her by now."

"We trust her," Raffi put in unexpectedly. "She wouldn't betray us."

Shean nodded slowly. "Is that so, girl?"

Carys looked at him, trying to keep her mind empty as she'd been taught. She felt strangely miserable. "Of course," she murmured.

"I hope so."

"Keeper," Galen said urgently, "can you do anything for me?"

Shean looked uneasy. Finally he said, "I will try. It depends on how deep your hurt was. Eat first. Then you and I will meditate, and try the healing." He looked at the others. "We will be some time, but there's plenty of food here. In the room beyond are beds, and water for washing. Make yourselves comfortable. You have come home, keepers."

The food was good. Raffi felt he hadn't eaten properly since leaving Lerin's village, and though Carys was quiet, she ate well too. The Sekoi picked delicately at fruit, spitting out pips and looking around the room curiously.

Later, when Shean and Galen were gone, they all slept, on small comfortable couches near the fire, and the Sekoi in a nest of cushions it had piled in one corner. Deep in the night, Raffi opened his eyes. Galen was standing in the warm darkness, looking into the fire.

Raffi propped himself on one elbow. "Did it work?"

But already he knew the answer. Galen gave him a look that went right through him; the keeper's face was drawn and exhausted.

"What does the keeper fear, Raffi?" he muttered hoarsely.

"Despair," Raffi whispered. "But Galen . . ."

"I know despair," the keeper said. "Despair and I are old friends."

"It's not your fault!"

"It must be. I have failed in some way. I have to pay and this is the way God chooses."

Raffi shook his head hopelessly. He felt like crying. "We'll find the Crow. The Crow will cure you."

Galen didn't answer. He sat in the chair, knees huddled up, staring into the flames. When Raffi went back to sleep, he was still there.

Journal of Carys Arryn
Date unknown

What's happening to me?

First I feel sorry for Galen, and now the old man's got me feeling guilty. This place doesn't help. It must be one of the last strongholds of the Order anywhere, and I should be glad that I've found it, but the whole thing seems . . .

CARYS STOPPED. Then she crossed out everything furiously and started again.

The Wounded City

They have a Relic-chapel here. I saw it this morning, though Galen spent most of the night in there. It is really very beautiful; Raffi was almost moved to tears. There are superb statues, so real they might almost be Flain and Tamar and the others. Candles burn before them. Relics are kept in boxes of gold—the Sekoi was squirming with jealousy. The windows are pieced together from broken fragments. Seeing it was strange. Old Jellie would have hated it, and so should I. It's just . . . the statues looked too real. I almost thought Flain was looking at me.

Superstition is easy to catch.

Now we're waiting for Shean. I think he has some idea where the Crow may be. If there is such a man.

SHE CLOSED THE BOOK and stuffed it away quickly as the old man shuffled in with Galen. They sat down. All at once it felt like a council of war, and Raffi's nerves tightened as the tension gripped him.

Shean began. He laid the small glass globe carefully on the table, his hand trembling slightly. "Galen has explained how you came to find this. I'm not sure, but I think I know what it is. I have spoken to him about it; that knowledge lies only between us, for now. It is a great relic, and if it is what I think, then it will lead you to the Crow." He looked uneasy. "If that is where you still wish to go."

Galen looked up, astonished. "Of course it is."

The old man paused, moistening his dry lips. "The House of Trees, keeper, if anything remains of it, is under the darkest, most dangerous part of the city. Those who have gone there have not returned."

"So you know where it is?" the Sekoi asked drily.

"We have . . . some idea. There is an ancient list of ways—a list of streets. It dates almost certainly from before the fall of the city. Others have copied it and, I presume, followed it. As I say, none have come back."

"You haven't tried?" Carys was surprised.

The old man's gloved fingers twisted together. "No. I feel it's important I am here. We must gather, find our scattered brothers, rebuild the Order. This will be our center—the heart of the network. We need you here, Galen. Stay with us."

Galen stared at him. "What about me? I need the Crow!"

"My son," the old man said softly. "Have you ever thought that there may be no Crow?"

"NO!" Galen leaped up, his face dark and wrathful. "Never! And how can you say that! Even think it! What has happened to your faith, old man? Has this city of horrors smothered it?"

Shean sat silent. Finally he said, "You may be right to rebuke me. I've lived here too long in the dark, Galen; seen too many martyrs, too many children dragged away. Under this room so many of their bodies lie, bought from the Watch, secretly buried. And maybe I've become weak. Maybe I've thought, if the Crow was here, would he not have saved us from this? Would he not have risen up and saved the city?"

"You sound like a Watchman!" Galen prowled in disgust, then turned swiftly. "Even in darkness, we have to believe! I've learned that. It's we who have to rise up, Shean, us, the remains of the Order! The Makers left the world to us, and if it's lost, then we are the ones who lost it! We have the power! We still have it! And he's waiting for us to find him, to come to him!"

In the silence that followed, the Sekoi said quietly, "Indeed, many of our stories say the same."

Shean shrugged. "Then I hope you find what you want. Because it tears at you so much I won't hold you back. I can give you the List of Ways, though you must swear not to let it fall into the enemy's hands. But think hard, keeper." He stood up and gazed across the room at Galen's grim face. "Are you doing this to save the Order? Or to heal your own loss? Would you be so eager to face death if you didn't think the Crow could cure you?"

Galen glared at him bitterly. "I hope so," he breathed.

"Of course he would," Carys snapped. They all looked at her in surprise; she felt a bit surprised herself, but she folded her arms and looked Shean in the eye. "He hasn't come all this way for himself. I've seen that. Nor has Raffi. They believe in this Crow, and if you'd had their faith you'd have gone to find him yourself, years ago. Keep the questions for yourself, keeper. Mightn't it be that you hide in here because you're too scared to go out?"

Raffi was grinning; the Sekoi smiled slyly. Galen's look was hard and strange.

Shean nodded slowly. "The Litany says the keeper is wise who knows the voice of truth. Maybe what you say is so." He sat down again, looking suddenly tired and older. His black fingers caressed the glass globe. "You go with him then, girl?"

"I've come this far."

"But you don't believe in the Crow?"

She hesitated, uneasy. "Maybe. I don't know. I'd like to find out."

The Sekoi nodded. "And so would I." It rubbed the fur on its face with one sharp finger. "It would interest us. We have our own ideas about the Makers."

"And heresy, most of them are," Galen growled. He came over to the table. "Let me have a copy of this list," he said quietly. "My friends and I will leave tonight." He paused, and the black and green beads glinted at his neck. "With your blessing, keeper."

Shean stood. "You have it, keeper. And maybe you

will be the one the prophecy speaks of. The one who will come back."

THEY LEFT AT NIGHTFALL, though in Tasceron night was eternal. Now they traveled light. Galen had left all the relics in the safety of the chapel; he took only the glass globe and the chart. They each carried a little food; Carys had her bow. The Sekoi went empty-handed, as before. It seemed able to go for a long time without eating; when Raffi asked how it would manage it just purred at him, "I could eat you, small keeper."

Raffi laughed, but uneasily. There were some nursery rhymes he'd heard from his mother . . . As if it knew, the Sekoi laughed too, a small, mocking, barking sound.

Shean's men went with them as far as a corner of a terrace, where a great set of wide steps led up into the dark. There one of them said, "This is as far as we go. Good luck, keepers."

Galen gave them the blessing; they melted into the shadows expertly. Watching them go, Raffi said, "Now we're on our own again."

The Wounded City

"We're never on our own!" Galen glared at him. "You've been neglecting your lessons, boy. While we go you'll repeat the whole Book to yourself, from the beginning to the death of Flain. Every verse, every prophecy."

Raffi pulled a face at Carys. She laughed.

But he could hardly concentrate on his task. They moved through inky streets; twice steam hissed up from under their feet, scattering them in terror. Sparks lit the sky far to the north. No one spoke. Galen led them, guiding himself by the small scrap of paper Shean had pressed into his hand, rubbing soot from the walls, hunting the shattered name plaques of the ancient streets.

When they came to the tunnel he was ahead of them.

"Down there?" Raffi came up and looked at it dubiously.

"Through it and left, somewhere. Do you feel any danger?"

"I told you, I can't feel anything here. Just the dark, and heat somewhere, something smoldering . . ."

They looked into the brick archway; inside it was black, with small gray lichens blotching the damp walls. Galen stepped in. "It seems empty. I can see to the end."

He took one more step and, with a sudden slash and clang that terrified each of them, an iron gate crashed down from the roof behind him, cutting him off from them. The tunnel rang with echoes. Somewhere ahead an eerie screaming rang out, wild and urgent. Raffi flung himself at the bars of the gate; he felt the Sekoi strain beside him.

"It won't move!"

Fiercely, Galen was tugging and heaving at the metal grid. Behind him came shouts; the wailing rose to a howling of skeats.

"Get out!" he yelled. "Take these! Quickly!"

Hastily he thrust his hands through the bars; Raffi snatched the chart and globe, but then he couldn't move, though the noise was piercing every nerve. "Galen . . ."

"Run!" the keeper raged. "Get away. Get him out of here!"

The Sekoi's fingers grabbed him. "He's right, Raffi!"

"We can't just leave him!"

"You have to." Galen's grip caught his. "You're the

keeper now, Raffi. Find the Crow. That's all that matters. Find the Crow!"

The darkness behind him was moving; men, hounds, a crack of blue light.

"The Watch!" Carys yelled.

"Don't worry," Galen said. He pulled upright, his hawk-face hard in the glimmer. "The Makers are with me, Raffi. We'll meet again. Now, get him away!"

Carys and the Sekoi had to drag him, sobbing and yelling. Behind them, blows and howls rang in the black tunnel.

The House of Trees

21

The Makers turned to Kest in despair.
"What have you done?" they cried.
"How have you betrayed us? Your
distorted birds, your hideous beasts
have marred our world." So they took
him and locked him underground for a
hundred years, without food or light.
And each time they looked in on him he
was silent and unsmiling.

Book of the Seven Moons

"HOW DO YOU FEEL, SMALL ONE?"

Raffi shook his head hopelessly. He was shaking and felt sick, though they had run through the streets till they thought they were safe. The Sekoi sat down by him. "Galen is a brave man," it said kindly.

"Yes." Raffi's voice was fierce. "I've seen him yell at a skeer-snake in the forest till it couldn't face him. That was before . . . But he can do anything. He's not afraid of danger." Choked, he closed his fists.

Its back against the ruined wall, the creature nodded. "It seemed to me that he sought death. He had a great

loss to bear. Now he will be a martyr for the Order. That
is a good thing, is it not?"

Raffi nodded. "So the Litany says." But his voice was
small and reluctant, and the silence after it bleak.

Carys flung down the pebble she'd been fingering.
"That's it. That's enough!"

"What?"

"I said, that's enough." She stood up and marched over
to them, kicking the rubbish in the cloister aside. "How
can you sit there and talk like this! Galen is no use to
anyone dead!"

"They believe . . ." the Sekoi began patiently, but she
waved at it angrily. "I know what they believe! 'The blood
of the Order benefits the earth'—all that nonsense! But I
don't! I say we should do something, not just sit here!"

"We will," Raffi said. He looked up, his face determined. "We'll find the Crow. Just like he said."

"But what about Galen!" She dropped to crouch by him.

"We can't help him. The Watch will torture him."

"They will if we don't get him out!"

The Sekoi stared. "From a Watchtower? Don't torment
the boy. It can't be done."

"Do you think I want to leave him?" Raffi muttered, despairing. "If there was any chance, Carys, any chance at all. But there isn't! No one can get into those places!"

She got up abruptly and walked to the edge of the cloister. Pinned on a row of broken pillars, a dead vine rustled. Owls hooted, far off in the stillness. Standing with her back to them, she said, "I can get him out."

After a second Raffi looked up. "What did you say?"

"I can get Galen out."

Raffi stared at the Sekoi in bewilderment. It stood up. "Explain," it said dangerously.

Carys turned around. She forced herself to look at it, but its eyes were yellow and sharp, and she couldn't face Raffi either.

"I work for the Watch. I'm a spy, and I have been from the beginning."

There was a second of intense silence. Then Raffi said, "Don't be ridiculous," but his voice was cold and he stared at her in growing horror.

She forced herself to meet his eyes. "I'm not. It's true."

"You can't be!" He jumped up so quickly the pile of

stones behind him slid down. "You've been with us all along! Your father—"

"I haven't got a father." She glanced at the Sekoi. "I was brought up in a Watchhouse. I came with you because . . . well, at first because I was hunting Galen."

"And then the Crow. You wanted us to get you to the Crow!"

"Raffi—"

"Don't speak to me!" He turned away, then helplessly swung back. "You used us! All that time you lied to us? All you told us about your father . . . ?" Choked with anger, he gripped his fists; to her astonishment tiny green filaments of light flickered around his fingers. "Carys . . ." Then he laughed harshly. "I don't even know if that's your name! I don't know who you are anymore!"

She bit her lip. He looked as if his world had crashed to pieces. "It is my name."

"Did you betray Galen?"

The Sekoi's question was icy; the fur of its nape had swollen and thickened.

"Of course not!" she snapped.

"But someone did."

"No. It wasn't like that."

"So you did betray him?" Raffi gasped.

"I had to get us into the city! Let me explain!"

"Why should I let you!" he raged. But then he sat down suddenly, as if his legs had given way, and his voice was bewildered. "I just can't believe this is happening."

Carys sat beside him. Her voice was dry and hard. "At the gate, when we hid under the wagons, I was caught. It was a hopeless plan. I told them who I was, that you were spies. They let us in. I swear I never said anything about relics, or keepers. I wouldn't have. I wanted the credit of your capture for myself."

Ignoring his look, she went on. "The news was passed on. But listen, Raffi, I'm sure they don't know who Galen is. That rat-trap was just bad luck; there are probably hundreds like that around the old citadel— aren't there?"

She glared at the Sekoi; it nodded, reluctant. "So we could get him out, Raffi; get him out before they realize who they've got!"

"But why? Why do you want to get him out? Why don't you go back to them and give them all the things you know—where the Sekoi live, the sky-road, Lerin, the Pyramid!" He sounded harsh, like Galen. "Haven't you gotten enough from us, Carys!"

"That's not it. I don't want Galen tortured."

"Might that not be because he may give them all the information you've worked so hard for?" the Sekoi asked acidly.

"NO! Why won't you listen! I like Galen. Like a fool I've gotten to like you all!"

She stood up, pushing back her hair, angry with herself. "I know you can't trust me now. If you want, I'll go away. But first I'm going to get him out, Raffi, and if I have to, I'll go by myself." Picking up the crossbow, she checked it over, her hands shaking.

Raffi stared at her. He felt bewildered, and utterly betrayed. He wished he could hate her, that it was that simple, but she was still Carys, still the same.

He looked at the Sekoi. "What should we do?"

"Your choice, small keeper. I'll stay with you, whatever you decide." It rubbed its furred face with one long finger.

"She may be able to get him out," Raffi said with difficulty.

The House of Trees

"She may. Or she may just be taking us back to them. More prisoners to her credit." It gazed at her, narrow-eyed.

Raffi stared down at his hands. He prayed, asking for knowledge, for the way to go, but his mind was as dark as the cloister, and the Makers were silent.

Then, without knowing he'd decided, he stood up.

"All right. We'll take the chance."

Carys smiled at him but he ignored that; he looked away, furious with her. "If you betray us . . . I still don't know if I should be trusting you."

"You never will know," she said, "until you do. Galen would tell you that."

He took out the chart. "Where do we go?"

"They'll have taken him to the nearest Watchtower. Is it on there?"

"There's one marked."

"That'll be it. Lead on, Raffi."

With a glance at the Sekoi, which shrugged, he turned uneasily away and crawled through the hole in the wall.

THE STREETS WERE A NIGHTMARE of dark smoke. Neither Raffi nor Carys was as alert as they should have been; if the Sekoi hadn't hissed a warning, the flock of draxi swooping over the turrets of one villa would have had them.

Confused, struggling to think, Raffi found himself going back over everything that had happened, trying to see Carys as a spy—on the downs, on the ship—but it hurt him like a pain and he blanked it out, concentrating only on the streets, their crumbling names.

Behind him, Carys was silent. She was angry with herself, defiant, reckless, hot. She didn't care what they thought. But she'd show them. Only she could get Galen out, and she'd do it, because she wanted to, because no one would bring him in except her.

In the alley opposite the Watchtower they crouched. At the end of the dark lane there was light, some hanging lanterns and a great fire that blazed on the cracked paving. Men were gathered around it; shadows, talking. Behind them, the great walls of the tower rose up into darkness, without windows.

"Now what?" Raffi said.

Carys eased the bow. "I go in. By myself. I'll tell them

some story—that Galen is vital to my mission, that I have to follow him to get . . . well, something important. I won't mention the Crow."

Raffi laughed bitterly, but she went on. "The trouble is, even if they believe me, they may not let me bring him out alone. That's where you come in."

"Us?"

"If Galen and I get out, we'll come down this lane. Hide somewhere, down under that broken arch. Let us go by; but if anyone follows, deal with them."

"Deal with them? We're not the Watch."

She grinned at him spitefully. "You know the Order's secrets, not me."

He didn't smile. But as she walked away up the alley he blurted out, "Be careful," as if the words hurt him.

"And be discreet," the Sekoi murmured.

She turned and looked at its sharp yellow eyes and laughed. "Oh, I will."

GALEN EASED HIS LEG a little more and felt the heavy chain clink. He was dizzy and bruised; blood had dried on his face, and his shoulder was a mass of pain. He looked around carefully.

For a long time he had wondered if they had blindfolded him, but gradually he had begun to see; there was a tiny window up a long shaft in the wall, and the gloom that came through it was barely light, but his eyes strained through it. He was in some enclosed space, not large. Stretching out his feet, he could feel the opposite wall; his back was against another. Carefully he tugged up the heavy chains and ran his hands over the stone; it wasn't straight. Curved, as if the dungeon was circular. Above him was blackness; he said some words softly and they echoed, as if it was high enough to stand. The darkness smelled of rats, ordure, filthy straw. The stones felt slimy and cold.

Galen smiled grimly to himself. He hurt, but he'd told them nothing, and he was sure they didn't know who or what he was. And yet this was only the start. He knew enough tales of the cruelty of the Watch, but he wouldn't think of them now. That would be foolish. Instead he straightened his back and closed his eyes. Simple chants came to him first, then all the prayers and litanies; he spoke them softly till it seemed to him the darkness was filled with words, as if they hung in the air like spirits. "And Kest was in the darkness a hundred years. How slowly sorrow entered him, how he mourned for the evil he had done, all the things of darkness he had brought into the world."

Galen stopped. The story was not the one for now. And he knew, suddenly, that he would need every ounce of strength and will to stand up to them, not to tell them all the secrets of the Order. Wincing, he dragged his fingers up to touch the awen-beads; the smooth surfaces rolled under his fingers.

"I am as empty without as within," he muttered grimly. Then he nodded. "Though maybe I have one chance. One chance Kest never had."

"WHAT'S GOING ON HERE?" The Watchsergeant pushed his way through the men. "What is it? Another prisoner?"

"She says she's a spy." The men stood back, and the sergeant's eyes narrowed. He saw a girl of about sixteen, brown-haired, dirty, a crossbow on her back. She fixed him with a straight look. "Are you in charge here?"

He grinned. "Who wants to know?"

Putting her hand down her neck, she pulled out something on a chain; tugged it over her head and gave it to him without a word.

He held it to the light; she saw his face change. "Come inside," he said somberly.

Going in under the main arch, she noticed the defenses: armed guards, three metal gates, floor-spikes. If they didn't let her walk out she'd be here forever. But she set her shoulders and held her head up. Why should she worry? She was one of them.

They made her wait a few minutes in the courtyard. Then the sergeant came through a small arch and beckoned. He led her down a stone passageway and knocked on a door.

"Come in."

The sergeant looked at her. Carys took a deep breath, put her hand on the latch, and went in.

It was a small room with a crackling fire in the hearth, and the castellan was perched on the edge of the table.

The House of Trees

"You brought this?" He held the insignia up so that it glinted.

"Yes," she said, coming up to him.

"What house?"

"MarnMountain, 547."

"When did you leave?"

"Three months ago."

"Your spymaster?"

"Jeltok. Old Jellie, we used to call him."

He nodded, wheezing a laugh. "Oh, I know." Getting up, he strolled to the fire, glancing back at her curiously. His sparse hair was graying; he was older than most of his rank. Shrewder too, she thought, with sudden misgivings.

He coughed and spat into the fire, rubbing his chest. "Your mission?"

"Surveillance. On a man called Galen Harn. A keeper."

His face glimmered with interest. "And?"

She sighed, sitting suddenly in the only chair. "Watchman, I've come a long way. I'm hungry and cold. And I'm on your side. You don't need to treat me like a prisoner."

For a moment he was still. Then he nodded, went to

the door, and yelled. Carys took off the crossbow and laid it carelessly on the floor. It was no good to her here anyway.

The man came back. "Food's coming. I'm sorry—force of habit. Welcome home, Carys Arrin."

She looked up at him and smiled.

22

We have been used by one of our own.
He has mocked us all this time.

Litany of the Makers

RAFFI CROUCHED DOWN behind the remnants of the wall. "No sign of her."

The Sekoi was silent, biting its nails.

Raffi put his hand in his pocket and touched the globe; it was almost warm and he pulled it out in surprise, but the glass was dull and dim. He held it to his eyes and stared in, trying to see something; then tried with his inner eye, but saw only darkness. It was the first real chance he'd had to examine it; Galen always kept it close. But it told him nothing.

The Sekoi looked up abruptly. "Listen, small keeper. I think we should go."

"Go?" Raffi was blank. "Go where?"

"Anywhere. Out of here." It knelt up, and he saw the pupils of its eyes were black slits in the dimness. Its hand caught his arm, the seven long fingers clutching tight. "All my instincts say this is a trap! She's gone to them. She'll bring them here! For us! Don't you see, Raffi, I don't think we dare trust her."

A tiny pang of terror went down Raffi's spine. He said hoarsely, "I can't believe she'd—"

"She already has! Long before she met you!" It sprang up, a lean, agitated shape. "My people know of these Watchhouses. They take children young, feed them, teach them, train them. For years. How can all that be taken out of her? She is the Watch, she thinks like they think, hunts like they hunt. She'll have seen things you can't imagine—have practiced cruelties and spite. Her sorna— her soul—will have been changed by that! Don't trust her, Raffi!"

Raffi sat still, though its fear terrified him, made him restless. "Yes, but what about Galen?"

"Galen is lost! And they'll make him talk."

"He wouldn't."

The Sekoi sat down. "He will," it said softly. "Everyone does, in the end."

Raffi couldn't answer. The helplessness and doubt swept over him again; he had no idea what to do. They should go, should run, and yet . . . part of him wanted to stay, to believe she'd come.

"We need to get to the Crow," the Sekoi urged. "The Crow was a great power. If he lives, he can help us. But we need to go now, Raffi, before she brings the Watch and they take the map and the globe! That's all they need!"

Raffi stared at it. Then he got up again and gazed down the dark, empty street.

"THIS IS ALL VERY INTERESTING," the castellan said, refilling her cup. "So this man Harn has knowledge of this relic . . . you didn't say what it was, by the way."

Carys smiled. "No. I'm not completely sure, and besides that—"

"You want to keep it secret."

"My orders are to be as discreet as possible."

He nodded. "I see. But look, Carys, we can get any information you want out of this man by our own methods. Not that he'd be much good to you afterward, of course." He sipped the sweet wine and looked at her. "Wouldn't that be easier?"

She pulled a face. "In a way it would. But it would break my cover—I've worked hard to be accepted by them, and now I think they trust me. No, I think it would be best if I helped him to escape." She raised an eyebrow. "If you agree, of course. He's your prisoner."

He paused a moment, stoking the fire with fresh coals, then turned and picked up the insignia, dangling the silver chain over his fingers. "Who am I to stand in the way of the Watchlords?" He handed it back to her, and she slipped it on, feeling the cold discs slide against her skin. "But there'll be a price."

She looked up sharply. She'd been expecting this.

"How much?"

"Half. Half of the reward for the keeper, and the others, and half of whatever they give you for finding this relic."

She thought briefly. "All right. I've no choice."

"Nor have I. We need to work together." He rubbed

a hand through his stubbly gray beard. "Now. This escape will need to be convincing." He thought for a moment, then stood up and went out, and Carys finished the wine in one gulp. Picking up her crossbow, she loaded it quickly and swung it under one arm. Then she picked some bread off the tray and crammed it into her pocket. When he came back she was waiting by the fire.

He looked pleased, and she knew he had his own plans ready. "The Watch must watch each other first." That had been Jellie's first lesson—all her life she had seen it; even in school, child had spied on child, reported anything, competed for the honor of it. She'd been one of the best. Now they'd be watching her, but that was all she had expected.

"We're ready. Here are the keys." He handed her a small ring. "I'll show you a postern gate which will be guarded by one man—shoot at him and he'll fall. It would be helpful if you missed; I'm short of men as it is."

She took the keys. "How did I get these?"

"You'll have to serve up that story. After all, you've been trained for it." He coughed again, a raw bark. "I'll be glad to get out of this rat-hole. The smog gets to you."

"You're leaving?"

"I hope so. I hope to buy promotion to some comfortable village. Somewhere the sun shines." He laughed harshly. "When I get the money."

Their eyes met. She smiled wryly. "Thanks for the food. Now show me the way."

GALEN PULLED HIMSELF UP as the key rattled in the lock. With both chained hands he pushed the long hair from his face, and winced as the light fell over him.

"Galen!"

She was inside in seconds, crouched by him. He stared at her. "Carys!" Then, convulsed by fear, he grabbed her. "Is Raffi here? He's not been caught?"

"No. No, he's fine. Keep still!" She was unlocking the chains; they slithered off and he rubbed his bruised wrists with relief.

"But how did you get in here? What's been happening?"

"I'll explain outside." She tugged the chains through the straw and grabbed his arm. "There's no time now.

The House of Trees

Follow me close; don't speak. Do what I do. Please, Galen!"

He looked at her as if he would say something, then nodded. She helped him up, but he pushed her off. "I can manage."

"Good." She put her head around the door. "Come on. This way."

The steps led up, around a damp wall. She climbed soundlessly, Galen a tall shadow at her shoulder. He was stiff and sore, but he moved carefully and, glancing back, she saw his eyes were alert. At the top of the steps was a dim corridor, pungent with smoke; from a guard-room nearby the sound of voices and the rattle of dice echoed. They edged carefully by; Galen caught a glimpse of the men inside, their backs to him. Then he was running down a passage, into another, and all the time neither of them spoke.

Then Carys stopped. Finger to lips, she jerked her head and, stepping forward, he saw around the corner a man sitting on a bench eating lumps of potato from the tip of his knife.

Beside him was a small, half-open door.

Galen glanced at Carys. She raised the bow. He gave a harsh smile and shrugged. Carys was surprised, but she turned at once and braced herself. He saw the bolt quiver; with a sound like a crack it was gone. The man sprawled on the floor.

Leaping over, Carys had the door open; she turned back and gasped, "Leave him!"

Galen straightened from the body. He pushed past her to the door and peered around it. The night was black, the narrow alley stinking with refuse.

"Where?"

"Straight on!"

He followed her up the lane, leaping piles of rubbish, the rats scuttling before them. Ducking around corners, they came to a low arch and raced under it; in the shadow she swung around and racked the bow again hastily.

"You think they'll be coming."

"When they find out." She glanced back, then tugged away from the wall. "Down here."

Turning into a ruined courtyard, they crossed it and scrambled through a hole in the wall to a wider street. She turned left. "Hurry!"

The House of Trees

They ran close to the wall, through the fog of darkness and the soft hooting of owls. Once Galen stumbled; picking himself up, he glanced back. Shadows moved in the entrance to the lane. He ran after her, his face dark.

They climbed over a roof-fall, then under a wide arch of stone.

"Come on!" She ran ahead but he caught up with her and grabbed her arm. "Wait!"

She looked back. "We can't! They're coming!"

"Where's Raffi?" Galen hissed. "Where is he?"

"I don't know!" She stared into the darkness under the arch. "He should be here! It was here I said . . ."

They could hear the Watchmen now; soft feet running.

"In the doorway." Galen pulled her in beside him and peered out.

Instantly the side of his face was lit with color; a vivid green flash that dazzled them both.

"What was that!" Carys gasped.

The keeper grinned wolfishly. "We call it the third action of the inner eye. Don't tell him, but he's quite good at it."

Gazing past him she was shocked to see the archway

spitting flame and sparks; for a few moments it fizzed and crackled and then went black, and she could see the bodies of two Watchmen lying still.

"Are they dead?"

"Stunned."

"How can he do that?" she marveled as the shapes of Raffi and the Sekoi came slithering up the broken street.

Raffi raced up to Galen and stood staring at him. "She did it," he said in a choked voice.

Galen smiled grimly. "Indeed she did."

Raffi touched the keeper's arm hesitantly. "We thought you were lost . . ."

Galen shook his head. "Always keep the faith, boy," he said gruffly. "Sometimes the Makers act in ways we could never imagine. Have you got the chart?"

"Here."

"Then let's go from here. Before more of them come."

Following the list of streets, they twisted between houses and past palaces whose windows were empty, and through whose halls the wind moaned uneasily. Rain began to fall; a black, oily drizzle. The city was changing; they were coming to the oldest part, the citadel, and the ruins here were of great temples and palaces, shattered by the terrible destruction. The darkness grew deeper, and more silent; even the rats and owls were left behind, and all they heard now was the sound of their own running, soft footsteps pattering in alleys and doorways, as if the city was full of ghosts that fled endlessly.

After half an hour, Galen stopped them. "Here," he gasped. "We rest here."

It was a small window; climbing through they found they were in the kitchen of some villa. An empty hearth was black with soot, and one table still stood, huge and immovable in the center of the room.

Galen crossed to the wall and sat down, easing his leg with a groan.

Raffi crouched beside him. "Did they hurt you?"

"Not much. They were just warming up."

Carys sat too, more slowly. She looked at Raffi, who bit his lip. The Sekoi stretched its legs out and scratched its fur. "Are you going to tell him, or shall we?" it said severely.

"I will," Carys muttered.

Galen looked up at her. "I should thank you, Carys.

I owe you my life. Maybe more, my honor as a keeper." Gathering the black hair from his face, he knotted it in the dirty string and looked at her, his hawk-face grim and dark. "It's a debt I'll pay, if ever I can."

"You may not want to," she said.

He frowned. "Why not?"

She was silent, looking down. Raffi rolled the glass globe nervously in his pocket.

"I've got something to tell you." But Galen looked at her so sharply that she couldn't say it; for the first time in her life she felt afraid to speak. Lies leaped to her mind, convincing stories, excuses; fiercely she drove them away.

When she did speak, her voice was defiant. "Galen, I've been deceiving you. I'm not what I said. I'm a spy. For the Watch."

It was out. His face did not flicker, his eyes black and keen. She looked away, but his answer made her jerk her head back in astonishment.

"I know," he said.

23

*Kest's creatures attacked them. But
Flain had a maze built before the House,
and the beasts and birds of nightmare
wandered in it and howled.*

*Then Kest arose, and wept. "The
damage I have done," he said, "I will
make good. The monsters I have made I
will destroy."*

*And he took up his weapons and
walked through them all into the dark.*

Book of the Seven Moons

THEY ALL STARED AT HIM IN AMAZEMENT.
Then the Sekoi gave a low purr of laughter.

"You knew?" Raffi gasped.

"From the beginning." Galen rubbed his leg calmly. "From the first time we saw her at the tree."

Carys was staring at him. "You couldn't have!"

"And as we went on I grew more certain. She writes an interesting journal, Raffi. You should read it."

"You . . ." She shook her head, disbelieving. "You deciphered it?"

"A few times." He smiled sourly. "I'm sorry, Carys, but you were the one who was deceived. I kept you with us because I knew you'd be useful. You could keep the Watch away from us; get us where we needed to go. So it proved. At the gates, for instance."

Bewildered, she sat down. The Sekoi was purring in ecstasy, all its fur bristling. "Wonderful," it murmured. "Wonderful."

"I made sure you went under the first wagon. I knew there was no real way into the city, but I thought you'd persuade them. I also thought you might be useful if any of us were caught." He rubbed his sore neck. "Luckily for me."

There was nothing, nothing she could say. The shock of it was like a cold downpour; it left her shivering. All this time she thought she had been so clever . . . She shuddered with the thought of her pride. All that time. Now she knew how Raffi must have felt.

He looked furious. "Why didn't you tell me?"

Galen glared at him hard. "Because I'm the master, boy. I keep the secrets. And besides, you'd have given it away a hundred times. You can't lie well enough."

Astounded, Raffi collapsed into silence. Galen leaned forward. "But I'm surprised, Carys, that you've already told these two. When I saw you in that cell I presumed you'd have pretended to be caught. So whose side are you really on?"

She was silent. They all watched her. Then she said quietly, "I'd only ever known the Watch, Galen, until I met you. I'd never spoken to keepers before. You did some things . . ."

He nodded, his long hair falling. "They told you it was all illusion."

"But why?" She looked up at him, face flushed. "I'm beginning to see some of the things they told us aren't true. I'm not sure anymore what I should believe. And then, when you were caught . . ." She shrugged. "I just wanted to get you out."

Galen looked at her, and something in his eyes softened.

The Sekoi squirmed uneasily. "Very touching," it muttered. "Forgive me for saying this, but, keeper, you realize this may all be lies. She may still want us to take her to the Crow. That's why she got you out."

"I do," Carys said.

"Yes, but only to solve your doubts? Or might you not

turn on us all when you find him? To capture the Crow would bring you a great deal of gold, no doubt." Its eyes gleamed yellow.

"For myself," she snapped.

"Prove it," Galen said quietly.

"How?"

"Leave your weapon here."

She stared at him, astonished. "That's madness! The city is full of dangers; we'd have no protection."

"Do it as an act of faith." His dark eyes watched her carefully. "Keepers carry no weapons."

"They do," she retorted. "Invisible ones."

"I have none, Carys."

She glanced away. "Yes, but just to leave it here! It's so stupid!"

"It will show us that you mean what you say."

She turned; for a long moment she stared at him, then at Raffi, who said nothing. Finally she pulled the bow off her back and threw it down. "I must be totally insane!"

Disgusted, she flung the spare bolts after it. "No wonder the Order's been wiped out!"

The House of Trees

"It hasn't. Not yet." Galen took the globe from Raffi and fingered it. "And it never will. Not while we have faith."

As he said it an enormous crack burst in the sky outside, making them all jump. The Sekoi slithered to the window; as it looked out, they saw its face was rippled with red light.

"You'd better see this," it hissed.

Raffi pushed in. Another whooshing sound shot up; he saw a burst of red flame high in the dark; it fell in flakes behind the high walls.

"What was it?"

"Watch-flares." The Sekoi pulled its head in. "They've found the men under the arch. We need to move."

"Carefully though." Carys followed. "They'll double the patrols."

She slid out behind the Sekoi, but halfway through the window Raffi saw her look back at the crossbow; a hopeless, bitter look. Then he climbed after her.

Galen hurried them. They moved through broken palaces like shadows. But soon the buildings were left behind; they came to a desolation of smoke, rising and hissing from cracks; shattered walls broke up the way.

There were no streets here; the destruction had left only tumbled masses of stone. They hurried by the smashed pieces of an enormous statue; Raffi saw a hand as big as a room, lying pointing to the sky and, still in its original place, a huge bare foot, so vast that the toes were like small hills they had to scramble over.

The stench grew. Shadows of draxi swooped overhead, their screams keen. Raffi slipped and slithered behind the others, glad that Galen had the globe; he had fallen so often he would have broken it.

Now they ran over a wide square, their feet scuffling on the stones, and in the middle came to a pillar so tall its top was lost in the black sky. Galen stopped to look at it; every side was covered with cryptic letters.

Raffi caught his arm. "We can't stop."

"Look at it. Centuries old. The secrets it has."

"Hurry!" the Sekoi hissed from the dark. "I can smell them. They're close!"

They raced across the square. On the far side was an inky stillness; plunging into it, Raffi heard Carys shout, then he felt the steaming water soak his knees. He scrambled back.

The House of Trees

"Flooded," the Sekoi spat.

They gazed at an eerie landscape. An archway and some broken pillars rose from the water. Vapor hung above the surface and some leathery vegetation had managed to sprout here; it grew over the broken walls like a creeping rash. Steam gathered around them; where they stood, the ground was reverting to marsh, stinking of sulfur and the invisible heat.

Raffi tugged his feet out.

"We'll have to go around." Galen glanced back. "Take care. The ground may not be safe."

They had reached the heart of Tasceron, and it was a morass of ruined halls. Here and there carvings rose, half a body, a broken face; strange obelisks and doorways that led nowhere, standing on their own in the dim lake. Carefully they made their way around the edge of the swamp, climbing over walls and through gaps and holes.

Finally Galen stopped. He bent over the chart. "We're close. We need to find a tree."

"Here!" The Sekoi looked around, wondering.

"Yes. A calarna tree."

Raffi stared at him. The calarna was the first tree, the

tree of Flain. It had given its branches for the House of Trees. Were they that close?

"Spread out." Galen crumpled the paper. "Quickly."

Turning, Raffi ducked under the wall into a blackened garden. Brambles were waist-high; he forced his way into them, arms up, dodging the swinging, slashing thorns. Then a stifled yell stopped him.

"Galen! Over here!"

Tearing his coat in his hurry, he backed out and found Carys at the stump of something warped and ill-shapen. Galen shoved her aside and bent down to it. He gave a hiss of satisfaction.

"This was it."

"Keeper." The Sekoi's voice was quiet and cold. They looked up at it; its yellow eyes were narrowed.

"We're being watched."

"Sense-lines, Raffi!" Galen growled. "Now!"

Silent, he sent them out, and touched the flickers of men, many of them, running silent as ghosts through the ruined arcades. Galen was on hands and knees, groping on the ground. "Hurry! It's got to be here! An opening of some kind!"

The House of Trees

A slither of stones behind them. The Sekoi's fur prickled.

"No time to look, keeper."

"We have to find it!"

Carys crouched beside him. "Should have kept my bow," she whispered.

Desperate, they groped hurriedly in the dark among the smashed wreckage of rooms; broken pots, cups, tiles, brick and mosaic, shards of glass that glinted in the steamy haze.

Digging a splinter from his skin, Raffi felt the sense-lines snap, one by one. "They're here!" he gasped.

"I don't care!" Galen roared. "Find it!"

Sweating with worry, dizzy with the effort of keeping the lines out, Raffi swept a clutter of rubble aside and saw with a leap of his heart a face in the mossed floor. It was a mask of beaten copper, a huge thing, riveted down, and on its forehead, almost trodden out, a ring of six small circles, and in the middle, the seventh.

"The moons!"

"What?" Galen was there; his firm hands on the mask, fingers stretched flat, feeling for marks and symbols Raffi couldn't see, pushing and prodding.

Behind them, a whistle sounded; another answered, far to the left.

Then a voice rang out, loud in the darkness. "Galen Harn! Listen to me!"

Carys's head jerked up.

"Galen Harn!" the voice roared again. "This is the end for you! My men are all around you, keeper, so come out and bring your friends with you. Don't try anything. We're all armed."

Galen's fingers stopped. Under his hands the slab had moved; with a hoarse whisper it lifted, just a fraction. Out of the black slit came a dry, musty smell.

"Get something," he muttered. "Heave it up!"

The Sekoi jammed a branch under; it splintered but was enough to heave the stone wide; below it they saw a hot steamy darkness that daunted them all till the castellan yelled again.

"Come out, keeper! Or we come in!"

"Down," Galen said.

Raffi slid in first, feeling Carys follow. There were steps; his feet found them and he went down fast, afraid of falling. Above him, bodies slithered, dust fell.

The House of Trees

Then the slab came down, and shut tight.

"Keep silent," Galen hissed. "Don't move!"

Around Raffi, the silence breathed. He could feel Carys's elbow in his chest; looking down he saw only blackness, but far down, something plopped into a pool, a tiny, far-off sound.

Muffled yells came from above. Something scuffed on the slab; Raffi had a sudden vision of a Watchman standing on it, and then he saw the man as if he was looking up from the ground through the eyes of the copper mask. He swayed, giddy; Carys grabbed him. She said nothing, but her clutch was tight.

The shouts and scuffs faded.

After a while Galen's whisper came down. "Go on, Raffi, as quick as you can. They'll find the entrance soon enough."

Spreading his hands, Raffi felt for the walls. He could only find one, to his right, so he kept his hand on that and shuffled down. It was hot and airless. The steps seemed wide, their edges broken and unsafe; as he went down and down, he waited for his eyes to get used to the dark, but all he saw was blackness.

His foot met floor. He slid it out carefully. There were no more steps.

"I'm at the bottom." His voice rang hollow, as if in a great well.

He waited till everyone was down, unable to see at all.

"We should have brought a light."

"Maybe we did." Galen's voice was close; he sounded pleased.

A glow loomed over Raffi's shoulder; he turned in surprise and saw Galen was holding up the globe. It glimmered faintly, a pale light that showed him Carys and the Sekoi's sharp face, lit with delight.

"How can you . . . ?" he breathed, but Galen shook his head. "It's not me. It will show us the way to go."

Something thumped, far above. Galen pushed past him. "Hurry! This way."

They realized they were in an extraordinary corridor, so narrow that the walls brushed them on both sides, so high the roof was lost in darkness. Galen walked ahead with the globe; it brightened as he went, throwing huge shadows on the walls. These were of some soft earth, and in them were deep slits, marked with plaques and carved symbols. Some were so high that Raffi realized the corridor floor must have been cut away, year after year.

"What are they?" Carys said.

"Graves," he said in awe. "The earliest Archkeepers were buried near the House of Trees. Think how old they are, Carys."

She nodded, but all at once he remembered she was one of the enemy, and was angry with her, and himself, and everything.

They came to a side tunnel; an identical corridor. Ahead, the way forked into two.

"This is the maze," Galen said abruptly. "Chapter fifty-six, Raffi."

He said the words aloud, without thinking. "For the way to the House of Trees is a maze of ways and choices. Let the wise man tread it carefully. He knows not where the last wrong turn may take him."

"And I always thought that meant something else." Galen shook his head and the green beads glinted at his neck. "But it's a real maze."

"How do we get through it?"

"The globe." Galen held it gently in the opening of each

tunnel; in the one to the left it seemed slightly brighter.

"We'll try here."

Following them down the slit, Carys muttered, "We ought to leave some trail. To get back out again."

The Sekoi snorted. "Yes, the Watch might like that.

"I suppose they might." It sounded as though she was laughing; Raffi glanced back and she winked at him. Behind her, the Sekoi looked unhappy. Troubled, Raffi hurried after Galen.

The maze was complex. They went as fast as they could, but the passageways grew even narrower, and there were so many of them leading off that Galen had to go a little way into each, watching the globe intently. Twice they took the wrong way, and had to go back as it dimmed.

Then from the back the Sekoi hissed, "Listen!"

Something moved, far above. A murmur of sound echoed. "They're in." Galen strode on quickly. "There's not much we can do about it."

Feeling the soft dust under his feet, Raffi knew the Watch would follow their tracks easily. All they needed was a lantern. He wondered if Carys had known that, and had been teasing him about leaving a trail. He didn't know. He didn't know anything about her.

Then he walked into Galen's back. The keeper lifted the globe. It was brilliant now, pulsing with white light. And they saw that the walls around them were no longer made of soil; instead they were strangely woven together; and as Raffi rubbed the dust off he saw that these were branches, hundreds of branches of different trees that had grown and tangled together. Galen held the globe high and they saw a vast doorway in front of them, its doorposts and lintel made of living calarna trees, black with age, and the mark of the Makers, the seven moons, was carved deep in the scented wood.

After a moment Galen began the words of blessing. Slow and sonorous, they sounded here; the old Makerwords, their meanings almost lost. Raffi made the responses, and the tunnels behind seemed to whisper the sounds back at him, as if all the dead remembered them. The Sekoi fidgeted restlessly, glancing back, and Carys stared up at the doorway as if inside it all her worst nightmares might come true.

Deep under the city, they had found the House of Trees.

The trouble was, Raffi thought, taking the globe from Galen, that they had also shown the Watch exactly where it was.

"Hurry," the Sekoi murmured.

The keeper went forward quickly and put both hands to the doors. He pushed hard, as if he expected them to be locked or swollen, but to their astonishment the wooden doors rolled smoothly back with a swish of sound.

And out of the House came light.

Blinding light.

24

We cannot undo his treachery. For once evil has entered the world, who can ever root it out?

Litany of the Makers

GALEN STRODE INTO THE BLAZE; coming after him, Raffi stared around in amazement. The great room was brilliant with cubes of light, standing on plinths against the walls. Everything was made of wood; the floor of smooth planks, and the walls of the branches of living trees that had grown and tangled in fantastic sculpture. How it had been done, he could not imagine. The scents of the wood were sweet and strong. He breathed them deep; they soothed him, like the forest at night.

All around, in strange arrangements, were relics; boxes of every size, dishes and plates of smooth strange materials, statues, pictures, books; a set of small shining discs that glimmered with a rainbow sheen as Galen held one up. Everything had been arranged, put on display, and among the relics were hundreds of half-burned candles with the mark of the Order on them. It was a shrine, untouched since the secret of it died with the last Archkeeper to have closed the great doors. And behind, coming from everywhere, a faint whine, almost too thin to hear.

"What are all these things?" Carys touched a plate.

"The belongings of the Makers," Galen said. She looked at him. His face was unsmiling, but inside he was exultant; it cracked his voice and lit his eyes. "This is where they lived. Flain's own house. The Order kept it as he left it, for always. This is the most holy place." He rubbed his face uneasily. "We profane it by bringing outsiders here."

The Sekoi glanced back. "Keeper, we need to close those doors."

As Galen took no notice, it ran back; Raffi went too. "Galen is overcome," the creature muttered. "He doesn't care. But I can't forget the Watch. Hurry, Raffi!"

Together they rolled the great doors closed, but there

seemed to be no way of locking them. Looking around hastily, the Sekoi caught hold of a heavy table and began to drag it. "Help me!" it hissed.

For a second Raffi paused, terrified to disturb anything; then he too tugged at the dark wood. After all, if the Watch got in, nothing would be left.

They jammed the table tight against the doors. Galen was watching. "It won't stop them." Then he turned. "Come and see this."

It was a picture in a book. Not a painting. A picture that was real. Raffi stared at it, his skin crawling with delight. He was looking at another world.

The sky was very dark, darker than possible, and in it hung a moon, only one, but enormous, with dim smudges of land and splinter-rays of bright craters. Around it, the stars shone in unknown patterns, frosty bright.

Hands trembling, Galen fumbled in other books. Images of animals, trees, birds, some like owls and bee-birds that they knew; but there were others that made Carys gasp aloud—great gray beasts, striped night-cats, a myriad of odd species bizarrely shaped, intricately colored, completely unknown.

The Sekoi chewed its nails. "Galen . . ."

"Another world," he said, rapt. "The world of the Makers!"

There was a crash at the door. The table shuddered.

Galen took no notice. His eyes had fixed on a small silver device on the table in the center of the room. He crossed to it and touched it in awe. There were five touch-panels, like Raffi had seen on relics before; these would operate it. Each had an unknown symbol, set in a circle, and above them were words: COMMUNICATIONS RELAY— OUTER WORLDS.

They were set on a panel, the shape of which made Raffi forget the pounding at the door and the hammering of his heart. A sign that was the most secret, guarded image of the Order; a black bird with spread wings, holding a globe.

The Crow!

Staring at it, he breathed, "But the Crow is a man!"

Something crashed against the door. Carys spun around.

"No. The Crow is a relic." Galen was still for a split second; then he grabbed Raffi and sent him sprawling back. "Block that door! Keep them out! Do whatever it takes!"

Feverishly his fingers danced over the panel.

Raffi and the Sekoi threw themselves against the table; they jolted it back and piled everything they could find against it.

"More!" the Sekoi yelled.

"There's nothing big enough!"

"Then do something." Carys grabbed his hand. "You can, Raffi!"

Closing his eyes, he threw force-lines around it, bound it tight with all the energies he could summon. As if the Makers lingered here, he found it easier than before; the very earth in this place was sacred, it gave him power, fed him, and he laughed aloud.

The door shivered; someone outside yelled in anger.

He ran back to Galen. "Is it working?"

"Not yet! Not yet!" Galen's face was tense; his fingers stabbed each symbol, working out sequences frantically. Behind him, the Sekoi crouched, its fur bristling.

Carys gripped the table. "Perhaps it doesn't work. It's too old . . . !"

"Be quiet! Pray, Raffi. Pray."

Galen didn't have to tell him. But the Crow was silent. No spark came from it, no flicker of life.

And then the room was humming. Amazed, they stared around. It was coming from everywhere and nowhere; it lay in the air and was full of distance; small crackles and hisses, a listening sound.

"Makers. Can you hear me?" Galen asked in a whisper.

Something spoke. It was the voice of a ghost, garbled, distorted in bursts of static. All they knew was that it had asked a question. Galen was shivering, pale with dread and joy. He gripped his hands together. "Hear me," he breathed. "We need you! Hear me, lords!"

Far away, eons away, the Makers answered. "*We hear you. Who is this? What frequency are you on?*"

Galen's voice was unsteady. "I am Galen Harn, of the Order. Masters, come back to us! The world is slipping into the dark. Tasceron is fallen; the Emperor is dead. Do you know what's happening on your world, lords? We need you! Come back to us."

A hiss of static. Behind them the door was jerking

open; chairs crashing down. Only the Sekoi glanced back.

When the voice came again it was broken, the words fuzzy and slow, as if spoken distinctly and urgently, over and over.

"*What . . . world? What world?*"

Galen made the sign of blessing. "Anara," he breathed. "Are there others?"

The answer was a crackle of noise. "*Wait . . . light-years. Are you . . . colonists?*"

Galen gripped the table. "Say it again," he pleaded. "What did you say? Will you come?" But the hissing faded out and died.

The Crow was silent.

Galen bent over it, his face dark, and then slowly he straightened, and his eyes met Raffi's.

"They said they would come. They said, 'Wait.'"

"I'm not sure . . ."

"They will, Raffi! I know they will!"

With a crack that turned Raffi sick, the force-lines exploded; the doors crashed wide, men leaped across the table.

Galen turned, standing in front of the Crow. The

Watchmen stared at him, then around, curiously; each had a loaded bow and they were all pointing at Galen. Dizzy, Raffi pulled himself up and watched the castellan shoulder his way through.

He was a gray, bearded man. He folded his arms and looked at them all in silence.

"This is a great day for the Watch," he said softly.

It was Carys who moved. She came out from behind the Sekoi and said irritably, "You took your time! Where have you been?"

Raffi stared at her with horror.

The castellan smiled. "We had some trouble. Been wishing we were here, have you?"

She shrugged and crossed to him. "They know about me. Things were getting a little difficult."

"So what have I missed?"

She turned around and looked at Galen, her face set and hard. "The keeper will tell you. Show them the Crow, Galen. Show them now."

25

The leaves of the trees shall cry out for joy, for behold, the stars have spoken.

Apocalypse of Tamar

ALEN STARED AT HER; their eyes met. He stepped back, until the Crow was on the table between them, and he spread his hands over it. For Raffi it was a moment of black despair. She had told them. It was all over.

Then the light went dim. The Watchmen looked around uneasily.

"Take your hands off that device," the castellan called sharply.

Galen looked up. His face was wild and triumphant. "Too late," he said.

The thought-bolts burst from him like fire; they

exploded among the Watchmen, who yelled and scattered and dropped their bows. Two turned and ran. The doors slammed tight.

"Pick those weapons up!" the castellan raged. He grabbed one, raised it, and shot the bolt straight at Galen. Raffi gave a strangled yell, but the bolt had already burst into brilliant flames of green and black; then it shattered, sending pieces crashing across the hall.

Astonished, the Watchmen stood still.

"Take their weapons," Galen said harshly.

After a second, the Sekoi pushed past him. It snatched the bows quickly from the men's hands, gripping them with its seven fingers, a wide, happy smirk on its face. Then it dumped the pile against the wall and stood over them.

"What . . . who are you?" the castellan muttered.

The lights flickered, turned green. Galen was standing upright above the device; power from it filled him, flowed from him; he was flooded with it, Raffi could feel it, a wild, exulting joy that surged out of him.

"*I am the Crow*," he breathed. His voice was raw and strange; in the brightness his eyes were black.

The House of Trees

Raffi found himself trembling, shaking with fear, his hands clutched in the sign of blessing. The Sekoi crouched beside him, one hand on his shoulder.

It was Carys who answered, tense with excitement. "How can you be?"

Galen was taller, his face dark and hooked. Energy surged through him in crackles and sparks of color; Raffi saw blue and purple and silver threads of it flicker through the dark. Immense shadow loomed behind him, seeming to rustle and flap.

"I am the Crow! I have been buried too long in the dark," he cried, and his voice was harsh, both Galen's and yet changed. "Now I arise and look, Anara, I have summoned your Makers back to you; through the darkness and emptiness I call them! In ships of silver and crystal they'll come, Flain and Tamar and Soren of the trees—even Kest will come—and they will dispel the darkness and scatter the towers of the Watch. This is the prophecy I make! This is the truth I speak! They have told me they will come, and no one will stand against them!"

He flung out his hands; the shadows jerked wide. All

around him the walls were hissing and sprouting; Raffi
saw that the trees were alive, growing, slithering out
leaves and fruit. The Watchmen called out, some of them
crumpled on the floor, terrified, and behind them the
great doors thrummed with a strange electric hum, and
the symbols on them glowed green and gold.

And then with a yell of delight, Galen made the seven
moons, and they came to him with sparks of power
out of the dark; Pyra and Agramon, Atterix, the pitted
face of Cyrax, Lar, Karnos, the craters of Atelgar. And
they moved in their right patterns—the Web, the Ring,
the Arch—and Raffi laughed aloud to see them, and
the Sekoi purred behind him, its hand clutching his
shoulder tight.

As if he could never tire of it, Galen poured out his
newfound power; he made sense-lines that snaked and
tangled, brilliant flashes of scents, rivers and rainbows of
energy that spurted and crackled and lit every one of the
thousand candles with one enormous roar of flame.

And then suddenly he was still, and the room shim-
mered and glinted into silence. The lamps flickered, grew
brighter. They saw they were in a room of leaves; millions

of fresh green leaves that smelled like spring, and yet fruit hung there too, and great helios flowers.

The Watchmen were lying crumpled up against the door. Carys sat near them. She seemed too astonished to speak, but she was awake, and as Raffi came toward her, she staggered up unsteadily.

"Are you all right?" he asked.

She nodded, silent.

Galen followed them. He looked tired, the crow-black hair hung to his neck, but the very air about him still seemed to crackle.

"How did you know?" He gripped her hands. "How did you know, Carys?"

Her eyes widened, as if his touch burned. "I don't . . . I'm not sure. I just . . . felt that you could."

"But you went over to them—" Raffi began.

"Don't be ridiculous. I had to do something. Did you think I meant it?"

"I don't know." He stared at her. "I don't know what you are anymore."

She glared back, furious. "Well, neither do I, Raffi! Everything was simple before I met you! Everything was clear! The Order were frauds and fanatics and the Watch were my family and I wanted Galen Harn, dead or alive!"

She stared down at her hands. "That's all gone now. Nothing's the same. If the Order's powers are real, the Watch has lied to me, to all of us. I've got friends there, good friends. I won't leave them to be made fools of."

"If you go back," Galen said quietly, "they may see your doubts. I think you should stay with us, Carys."

She looked at him, a long, hard look. Then she hugged herself with her arms and said, "I can't."

"Keeper, you can't let her go back," the Sekoi put in, getting up from its corner. "Her or any of them. They've seen where your holy place is."

"I have the power," Galen said softly, "to wipe that from their minds." Ignoring Raffi's stare, he said, "And for the men I'll do that. But for you . . ."

Stepping forward, he faced her. "Now it's my turn to make an act of faith. Keep the knowledge. It will work inside you, Carys. It will draw you back to us. One day."

Wanly, she smiled. "Always trying to convert the fallen, Galen."

He nodded. "But come soon. The Makers will arrive, and I'd hate them to find you with the Watch."

"The Watch are my father and mother." She shook her head. "Or I thought so. But I can't wipe that training out. I need to think about things, find out what's true."

"You never will. But ask your questions carefully. If they think—"

"I know." She pulled a face. "I've seen people disappear. I know what happens to them, better than you."

He looked at her for a moment with a look that was new to him, then turned away. Bending over the Watchmen, he said something, and to Raffi's surprise they all stood up, but there was no consciousness in them, no memory.

"Lead them through the maze," he said to the Sekoi. "They'll follow you.

"Keeper . . . !"

"Don't worry. They're not dangerous."

With a wry grimace at Raffi, the creature shrugged and turned. The doors opened and the Sekoi walked through, the Watchmen following in a cowed, obedient huddle. None of them looked back.

Galen glanced around. "No power is left here. But the House will be sealed, and the secret kept." He glanced at Carys. "No one must know."

"Oh, don't worry," she said, picking a crossbow off the pile. "They'll only get it out of me on the rack."

"It might come to that," Raffi muttered.

He followed Galen through the doors, with one look back at the room of leaves, and then trudged thoughtfully through the maze. At one corner he turned and waited for Carys.

"I wanted to say I'm sorry." He felt awkward. "But I'm confused. Whose side are you really on, Carys?"

She caught his arm, swung him around, and pushed him ahead of her. "My side. And that's where I stay till I've decided." He felt her grin at his back. "You'll have to be satisfied with that."

He turned, blocking the way. "If you betray him, I'll hunt you down myself. I'd never forgive you."

Silent, she nodded. "I know," she whispered.

He walked on, grim, wondering if it was true, or if she would go straight to the Watch and tell them everything. Galen thought not. Galen with all his powers back—and

more. Galen, who had been the Crow, and had proph-
esied the future of the world.

"We'll have to write this down," he muttered.

"What?"

"Nothing." Coming to the stairs he ran up in the dark,
suddenly happy. "Nothing."

Outside in the dim square the Sekoi sat impatiently on
a low wall, chewing its nails. The Watchmen stood near,
an eerily silent group.

It leaped up in relief. "What have you done to these
men, Galen? Are they alive?"

Without answering, Galen faced the Watchmen.

"Go back to your tower. Remember nothing of what
you've seen. Forget me, forget these others, forget the
name of the Crow. Remember only that in your hearts
you fear the Makers."

They simply turned and walked away, the castellan
among them; for a long while the echo of their footsteps
rang in the empty alleys.

When they were gone Galen closed down the stone,
and then he and Raffi threw every hiding-spell they knew
around it, binding it tight, darkening it, until even Carys

realized that when she looked at the stone she could no longer quite see it, as if some blind spot hovered behind her eyes.

Finally Raffi looked around. The ruins of Tasceron were dark with smoke. Streets away, an owl hooted. "I almost thought all this would be changed."

"Not yet." Galen dragged his hair back irritably. "But when they come, we can rebuild this. We can rebuild everything."

The Sekoi stroked its fur. "You seem very sure of that, keeper."

Galen stood a moment, as if looking deep inside himself. Then he said, "I am."

They walked slowly over the broken stones to a splintered archway. The alley beyond was silent and black.

Carys turned suddenly. "I'll go on from here alone."

"Change your mind!" Raffi urged abruptly.

She grinned at him. "Look out for me. If the Makers do come, put in a good word." Taking the small pack off her back, she tugged something out and pushed it into his hands. "You'd better have this. You can keep it to remember me."

The House of Trees

And she was gone, a flicker in the shadows of the alley, and they could hear her feet running after the tread of the Watchmen.

Raffi looked down; it was a small blue book full of scrawled writing. "Good-bye, Carys," he murmured, and then sent one long sense-line curling after her.

"I can't help thinking," the Sekoi said drily, "that she's gone back there knowing everything she set out to know. I hope you're sure of what you're doing, Relic Master."

Raffi was silent. It was Galen who answered. "Faith is a strange tree. Plant the seed and somewhere, sometime, in the right weather, it will grow. We also have done what we came for." He turned to the creature. "We go back to the Pyramid. Then we need to get out of Tasceron. Can you help?"

The Sekoi's sharp face smiled. "I'm sure it can be arranged."

"Good."

"And then what? Do you drag me kicking and squealing back to Alberic?"

Raffi looked up. "Alberic! He's still got our blue box!"

Galen and the Sekoi gazed at each other with a strange glint in their eyes. Carelessly the Sekoi kicked a loose stone. "I suppose we could always steal it back."

"I suppose we could," the keeper said grimly. Then he grinned. "I think it's our duty really, don't you?"

THE SERIES CONTINUES IN

Book 2: **THE LOST HEIRESS**

THE STRAIN ON HIS ARMS was agony. Clutching the rope, he hauled himself up, hand over hand, gripping with aching knees and ankles.

"Hurry up!" The Sekoi leaned precariously from the tower ledge above, its seven fingers stretching for him. Behind it the Maker-wall glimmered in the light of the moons.

Raffi gave one last desperate pull, flung his hand up, and grabbed. A hard grip clenched on his; he was dragged onto the ledge and clung there, gasping and soaked with sweat.

"Not bad," the creature purred in his ear. "Now look down."

Excerpt from THE LOST HEIRESS

Below them, the night was black. Somewhere at the tower's smooth base Galen was waiting, a shadow with a hooked face of moonlight, staring up. Even from here Raffi could feel his tension.

"Now what?"

"The window." Delicately, the Sekoi put its long hand out and wriggled it through the smashed, patched pane. A latch clicked. The casement creaked softly open.

The creature's fur tickled Raffi as it whispered, "In you go."

Raffi nodded. Silently he swung his feet in and slithered over the sill, standing in the still room.

In the moonlight he sent a sense-line out, feeling at once the tangled dreams of the man in the bed, the sleeping bodyguards outside the door, and then, as he groped for it, the bright mind-echo of the relic, the familiar blue box.

It was somewhere near the bed.

He pointed; the Sekoi nodded, its yellow eyes catching the light. Raffi began to cross the room. He knew there was no one else here, but if Alberic woke up and yelled, there soon would be. The tiny man seemed lost in the vast bed, its hangings purple and crimson damask, heavy and expensive. Beside the bed was a table, a dim shadow of smooth wood, and he could just see the gleam of a drawer-handle. The relic box was in there.

Galen's box.

Inch by inch, Raffi's hand moved toward the drawer.

Alberic snuffled, turned over. His face was close to Raffi now; a sly face, even in sleep. Soundlessly, Raffi opened the drawer, pushed his fingers in, and touched the box. Power jerked through him; his fingers clenched on it and he almost hissed with the shock. Then it was out, and shoved deep inside his jerkin.

Glancing back, he saw the Sekoi's black shape breathless against the window; behind it the stars were bright. He backed, carefully.

But Alberic was restless, turning and tossing in his rich covers; with each step back Raffi felt the dwarf's sharp mind bubbling up out of the dark, a growing unease. As he turned and grabbed the window he felt the moment of waking like a pain.

Alberic sat bolt upright. He stared across the dark room; in that instant he saw them both, and a strangled

Excerpt from THE LOST HEIRESS

scream of fury broke out of him. In seconds Raffi was out, slithering down the rope after the Sekoi, so fast that the heat seared the gloves on his hands, and as he hit the bottom and crumpled to his knees he heard the dogs erupt into barking and the screeching of Alberic's wrath.

Galen's hand grabbed him. "Have you got it?"

"Yes!"

The dwarf's head jutted from the high window. "Galen Harn!" he screamed, his voice raw. "And you, Sekoi! I'll kill you both for this!"

He seemed to be demented with rage; someone had to haul him back inside. "I'll kill you!" he shrieked.

But the night was dark. They were already long gone.